"Hey, Noah?"

The man paused. Then two forest green eyes were on her.

"Yeah?"

"Don't let the belief that you know the people who live here cloud the fact that one of them could be responsible for what's happened. Knowing someone doesn't mean they aren't capable of violence, malicious intent or even murder. Sometimes the people closest to us are really only there to hide in our blind spots."

The pain that hadn't left in over two decades was a constant reminder that there were some things so low that not even light could touch them. "We need to catch who did this and that starts with that list. Amish or not, someone here has to have an idea of who might be behind it or at least a theory."

Noah took off his cowboy hat and thumped it against his chest, almost like he was saluting to her, though there was no pageantry in his answer.

Only a hard rumble that stirred something else within Carly.

"I'll do my best. You have my word."

TOXIN ALERT

TYLER ANNE SNELL

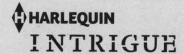

This book is for Julie Anne. I love our powers of being awkward.
May we always use them for good.

Special thanks and acknowledgment are given to
Tyler Anne Snell for her contribution to the
Tactical Crime Division: Traverse City miniseries.

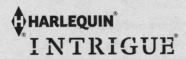

Recycling programs
for this product may
not exist in your area.

ISBN-13: 978-1-335-13687-9

Toxin Alert

Harlequin Enterprises ULC
22 Adelaide St. West, 40th Floor
Toronto, Ontario M5H 4E3, Canada
www.Harlequin.com

Printed in U.S.A.

Tyler Anne Snell genuinely loves all genres of the written word. However, she's realized that she loves books filled with sexual tension and mysteries a little more than the rest. Her stories have a good dose of both. Tyler lives in Alabama with her same-named husband and their mini "lions." When she isn't reading or writing, she's playing video games and working on her blog, *Almost There*. To follow her shenanigans, visit tylerannesnell.com.

Visit the Author Profile page at Harlequin.com.

CAST OF CHARACTERS

Dr. Carly Welsh—As the Tactical Crime Division's specialist in biochemical terrorism, this agent is put in charge when a biological attack is carried out against an Amish community. But because of a secret she's kept buried for years, the case might be harder than she thought. Can her civilian partner help her figure out who's behind the attacks? Or will both of their pasts work against them?

Noah Miller—After leaving the Amish when he was sixteen, this rancher has led a solitary life not far from the community. He might be labeled an outsider by the Amish now, but he's also the only one they'll talk to about the case. It's not what he wanted, but he can't deny that finding justice for the innocent while working alongside Carly more than has its appeal.

Selena Lopez—Carly's closest friend on the team, this TCD agent's specialty is in surveillance, tracking and suspect apprehension. She's also their K-9 handler.

Aria Calletti—TCD agent and former rookie of the team, she's fluent in multiple languages and known for taking down tough if not impossible culprits.

Max McRay—TCD agent and a veteran, he's the team's explosives expert.

Axel Morrow—Supervisory special agent of the TCD, he's the team's criminal profiler.

David Lapp—After being exiled for breaking church rules, this nineteen-year-old might just have an ax to grind with the Amish community.

Caroline Ferry—This wealthy real estate developer has to scrap her grand plans when three Amish families refuse to sell their land and not everyone is happy with the outcome.

Prologue

Noah Miller slipped his hands into his pockets, squared his shoulders against the cold and counted the bodies in silence. On a normal day he'd be the first to tell you that he didn't think Potter's Creek had a spot of ugly in it, but today? Today wasn't normal.

Today wasn't right.

And he'd guessed as much before he had come out to Amish country at the invitation of his father. A rare occurrence on its own, but nothing compared to what they were looking at on the Yoder farm.

"Twenty-four." Samuel Miller's voice was a shock against the cold quiet. Samuel nodded in the direction they were already facing. "Twenty-four cows dead," he repeated. "Make sure you don't touch anything."

Noah hadn't been planning on it but didn't say as much. He and his father hadn't been on good terms since he'd left home when he was sixteen. Now, twelve years later, they lived in the constant strain of their differences. Noah was just whom his family and their community called with an emergency, and that was still a hard pill for some to swallow. He might live only a mile from where they were now standing but that mile was the difference between the Amish world and the English world. And that difference was enough.

"What do you think it is?" Noah asked. "Poison? A virus? I've had a few cows pass on my farm before from sickness but I've never seen anything on this scale."

Out in the pasture was a sea of death. Not at all what he'd expected when he'd seen the number for the community phone pop up on his caller ID that morning.

His father hesitated. Not a great sign for an already dark situation.

"I don't know but it gets worse." Noah's brow rose at that. His father let out a long, low breath then nodded to the barn next to the pasture. "Isaiah is inside the barn. There are black sores on his arms."

"Black sores?"

His father nodded, solemn. Noah's confusion at being called out to meet him was swiftly hardening into a deep, terrible sense of foreboding. Isaiah Yoder, a loving father of five and a good guy, owned and worked the farm. Black sores on his arms and dead cows in his pasture?

This was bad.

This was very bad.

"The Haas farm lost ten cows a few days ago," his father continued, surprising Noah. "David and his sons who worked the fields became sick but then recovered. They believed it was a virus they picked up from the cows or something in the soil. Now I'm afraid that with these black sores it's something else. Something that could endanger the entire community."

Noah might have been estranged from his family but he still knew when his father was afraid. He could read it in the set of his shoulders and jaw, and hear it beneath a tone he was trying to keep even.

And he didn't blame him one bit for it.

"Whatever it is, it's bad," Noah spelled out. "We need to take Isaiah to the hospital."

His father shook his head. Fear was no match for being set in his ways.

"The Englisher doctor is in the barn examining him now."

Noah had every intention of continuing to insist but movement from the same barn pulled at their attention.

A balding man with large-framed glasses and a crease of worry along his brow stepped outside. When he saw them, he waved them over, shutting the door behind him, a palpable nervousness in his gestures.

"It's never good when the doc is nervous," Noah muttered.

His father didn't say a word as they walked over to greet the man. He introduced himself to Noah as Carson and then apologized for not shaking his hand.

That was a giant red flag to Noah even before the man got right to his point.

"It looks like Mr. Yoder is suffering from anthrax poisoning," he started, not pausing for any reactions. "In itself that's not necessarily a scary thing—anthrax poisoning can occur naturally in soil and infect cows and people—but, well, come look at this."

Noah and his father followed the doctor to an outside corner of the barn. He stopped by a pair of worn, brown work boots.

"These are Isaiah's boots. He was wearing them when I got here." Carson bent down and, without touching them, pointed between the heels. A dusting of white powder could be seen on each. "And this is what I believe to be anthrax."

Noah and his father were far from being in sync since he'd left the homestead but, in that moment, both Millers took a horrified step backward.

"As a bacterial infection, anthrax isn't contagious," the doctor continued. "But inhaling the powder? That can be lethal."

"But where did it come from?" his father asked. "Somewhere in the field?"

The doctor shrugged.

"That would be my best guess. Though, that's maybe not what worries me most."

Noah could see his father trying to work out what the doctor was referring to, but Noah already knew.

"Does this mean that someone put the anthrax in the field intentionally?" Noah asked. "And, if so, why?"

"Good questions, son," the doctor said.

They let those thoughts mingle in with the cold around them for a moment. No one had to say out loud that their morning had gone from one of worry to something much more.

Why would anyone put anthrax in the cow pastures on purpose?

Why would anyone target the Amish community like that?

Another flash of movement pulled Noah's attention away from his current thoughts, back toward the dirt road that led from the Yoder farm to the main one.

Someone was running toward them. A teenager.

And he was terrified.

Noah's adrenaline spiked at the sight. He started to run toward the boy, his father and the doctor behind him. When they met him next to the pasture's fence, he glanced at the dead cows without an ounce of surprise and then put his hands on his knees to try to catch his breath.

"What's wrong?" Noah hurried. "Are you hurt?"

The teen shook his head and then pointed wildly behind him.

"No, but my—my father and brother need—need help," he panted out. "They—they collapsed in the pasture at our farm."

Noah shared a quick look with the doctor.

"We need to get there now."

While his father had never liked riding in anything but horse-drawn vehicles, he didn't push back as Noah herded everyone into his truck. Instead, he got into the front seat and directed him to the farm of the boy's family while the doctor asked the teen questions in the back seat. However, when Noah cut the engine next to the cow pasture fence, his father became quiet.

"Doc, let's go," Noah said, another surge of adrenaline going through him. "Dad, you two stay in here."

Noah didn't have time to be surprised that his father listened. He and Carson hurried out into the field with purpose and caution.

Neither did them any good.

The father and son weren't unconscious on the grass. They were dead. Black sores on their bodies.

Noah kept his back to his truck after Carson confirmed there was nothing he could do. The two were gone.

But there were still people they could help.

"Isaiah needs to go to the hospital," Noah reiterated, voice low. "I think Mrs. Yoder will agree to that now."

Carson nodded.

"And I need to call the CDC."

He shared a look with Noah and said what Noah had circled back to thinking.

"I don't understand why anyone would do this. Especially here."

Noah gritted his teeth.

"Neither do I," he said. "But I sure as hell intend to find out."

Chapter One

Dr. Carly Welsh was in her chair less than thirty seconds before Director Alana Suzuki was in the briefing room, coffee in hand and disgust written across her face. She had been the big boss of the FBI's Tactical Crime Division since Carly had started working there three years before and, because of the team's closeness, Carly was able to register her expression now as a warning. Her news wasn't good.

Not one bit.

Then again, the cases that came to their team were never sunshine and daisies.

"There's been an attack on several farms in the small Amish settlement at Potter's Creek," she said in greeting. She motioned to the TCD tech guru, Opaline Lopez, in the corner of the room.

Opaline adjusted her neon green flower hair clip with one hand and activated the viewing screen with the other. The familiar mechanical whirl preceded the digital screen lowering at the front of the room. All five agents around the long table sat at attention, Carly included. The TCD's liaison, Rihanna Clark, and Alana's

administrative assistant, Amanda Orton, came into the
room and sat before the screen finished extending. Both
had tablets in their hands but both turned their full focus
on the first slide.

What came on screen wasn't exactly what Carly had
expected to see when she'd been called in that morning.

"Are those dead cows?" Selena Lopez, Opaline's
younger sister and Carly's closest friend, asked from
the seat next to her.

Everyone on the team had a specialty. Selena's was
surveillance, tracking and suspect apprehension, but it
was her love for her partner that colored her tone concerned at the moment. Blanca was a beautiful white
German shepherd who helped on just as many cases
as the rest of the team. She was the reason Selena was
an avid animal lover. Right now Blanca was no doubt
lounging in her dog bed in Selena's office a few hundred feet away from them.

Alana nodded and gave them a second to pass over
the picture once more. It was a beautiful landscape of
white and green and a picturesque barn in the distance.
Definitely not like any place Carly had seen in Traverse
City, Michigan. Sure, they had the bay, but the simple
picture captured the beauty *of* the simple. It reminded
her of the many trips she'd taken with her adoptive parents to St. Joseph County.

Except for the alarming number of dead cows.

"Twenty-four to be exact," Alana continued. "At first
it was thought to be something in the soil affecting this
one farm but—"

She motioned to Opaline, who clicked to the next

slide. She scrunched her face and pushed her pink-tipped hair over her shoulder. As if the movement would distance her from the death they were seeing on the screen.

Another picture of an otherwise beautiful scene showed more dead cattle. That picture turned into several more.

"—two other farms in the community were affected." Alana wasn't a person for dramatic pauses. In fact, she was straight to the point in every facet of her job. Yet, when Alana's gaze swept the group, Carly thought she stuck to her a moment longer than the rest. "And then there's this."

When Opaline switched to a new slide, Carly realized why.

It was a close-up of an arm. The black sores on it stood out in absolute contrast to the tan.

Carly had seen it before.

"Anthrax," Carly said.

Max McRay, their resident explosives expert and Army veteran, shook his head. Not because he didn't believe her but because any form of warfare triggered an automatic reaction. Carly had noticed that, sometimes when he was reminded of his service, he would shift his left leg and the prosthetic attached beneath the knee.

Carly hadn't been to war but poison? Well, when it came to personal hells, that was her trigger.

And Alana was the only one in the room who knew why.

"The doctor on scene noted white powder on this man's work boots—" Alana said, motioning to the picture "—and then was called away to a neighboring farm, where they found the bodies of a father and his son. They'd been feeling ill for days, but thought it was flu and still tended their farm."

Opaline switched slides.

Aria Calletti, the former rookie of their team, shook her head along with Max. Both were parents. Aria had met the love of her life on another case the team had closed, which she'd helped solve with her expertise in drug-running.

"This is when the doctor called in the CDC. They confirmed, as Carly said, anthrax was spread across each farm's pastures. Animals in the area are now being vaccinated, and mitigation efforts are underway."

"It was deliberate," Carly made sure to emphasize.

Alana nodded.

"It was deliberate."

The slide changed to the quick facts about the town with an aerial shot. Potter's Creek was small, mostly Amish, and was under the jurisdiction of an even smaller police department and a sheriff's department that supported three other towns. Basically, no one in town had the means or know-how to deal with such a malicious attack.

Which is usually when the TCD were called in.

The last of their team finally spoke. Axel Morrow had been promoted to Supervisory Special Agent when Alana had been promoted to Director five years prior. Although he was quick to remind them that he wanted to be viewed as part of the team and *not* the leader, there were moments when authority shone through his words.

"Which means we need to find out who's behind the attacks sooner rather than later."

"Agreed." Alana found her gaze again. Carly was hyperaware of her own stillness. Everyone on the team had a set of skills, an expertise. One such person was Axel. He was a top-notch profiler and a damn near impossible man to beat at poker. If anyone was going to pick up on her slight change in behavior it was him.

Then again, considering Carly had a PhD in biological warfare and defense, it stood to reason her discomfort had everything to do with the case.

And not a past she'd tried to keep secret since she was eleven.

"Since Carly's specialty is in biochemical terrorism, she will be lead agent on this," Alana added.

Then she opened the floor up to questions.

"There's no way it was something they contracted from the soil?" Selena asked. "I mean I've heard that anthrax can occur naturally, right?"

"This wasn't natural," Carly answered. She put her hand around her coffee mug but made sure not to stare into the drink. "Powdered anthrax spores don't just appear coating pastures. Someone put it there."

"Who would bother the Amish?" Max shifted in his seat again. "It's not like they're out there living fast and hard with questionable acts of indecency."

Aria thumbed at her engagement ring and tilted her head, thoughtful.

"Maybe it was an inside job," she said. "Someone from the community with an ax to grind. We all know vengeance can be a powerful motivator."

Opaline shook her head.

"One of the basic tenants of their religion is pacifism to the extreme," she pointed out. "They're strictly conscientious objectors to all things aggression, violence and war. They even go as far as avoiding any and all involvement with the military. They're famously not in the murder or vengeance game."

"But they are into shunning," Axel jumped in. "Those who leave or break their faith get the big boot out of the community to fend for themselves. We could be looking for someone who left trying to retaliate for being forced out."

"And they're human, after all. They could have a sociopath in their midst," added Selena.

That quieted the room as they all mulled the possibility.

Carly looked at her cell phone on top of the table. She had often admired the Amish's self-control when it came to living a more simple life. She could no more leave her phone behind than she could say goodbye to her high-tech apartment downtown. Yet the Amish made every decision with their virtues of simplicity and humility in mind.

And now someone had poisoned them?

If it wasn't an outsider, then the community of Potter's Creek was about to be rocked tenfold.

"We can talk more about religion and possible motives in transpo. We leave in two hours," Axel said, standing. He and Alana shared a look. They'd no doubt already had their own briefing before this one had started. He gave them all a sweeping smile. Like him, it was filled with boyish charm. It lightened the mood. "And I suggest no one wear their good shoes."

Opaline lightly laughed from behind her laptop.

"You heard the man, Selena," she said, looking at her sister. "That means you might want to holster any heels over three inches. I don't think Lous pair well with mud."

While it was common knowledge, and conversation, that Selena had a penchant for heels, the lighthearted tease clearly didn't land the way it was intended. Selena stiffened at Carly's side. She rallied a smirk.

"If you were in the field with us you'd know that my heels kick just as much ass as I do."

Her snark pulled a sigh right out of Carly before Opaline could pivot a comment back.

"You know, I bet Amish siblings don't snip at each other," she said. "That's part of their tenets you two might learn from."

"The Amish don't have a sister like Opaline," Selena muttered.

Everyone heard it. Opaline grinned.

"You're right. I'm one of a kind and don't any of you forget that."

The slight tension broke in the room. Carly felt the warmth of the coffee against her palm. She wanted to take a drink but stopped herself, readjusting in her seat to try to hide the redirect. One look at Alana, whose eyebrow was arched in question, and Carly knew the first moment the two were alone she'd go maternal on Carly.

But now wasn't the time.

Alana addressed the team one last time before calling the meeting to a close.

"Since the community is off the public power grid, there's only one building in town that has non-gas lighting and a phone. It's their community barn and where you'll set up for the duration of the case. And since the Amish typically aren't fans of outsiders, especially law enforcement, the area doctor who originally diagnosed the anthrax has recommended you rely on local Noah Miller as a liaison. He's a former Amish farmer who lives on the outskirts of Potter's Creek, close to town."

Former Amish?

Carly's eyebrow rose at that.

Opaline clicked to the last slide.

Intense.

That was the first descriptor that came to mind at the man staring back at her.

Tall, broad-shouldered, he was a man who worked manual labor and it showed. He wore a cowboy hat, a durable jacket, dark jeans and boots. If his dark hair couldn't be seen waving down to his chin, messy beneath the black hat, he would have looked like the poster boy for farmers of America. Someone who you, on reflex, pictured in your head when you thought of cowboys, too. Yet Carly had always imagined cowboys to be charming, outwardly hospitable people, and that wasn't the vibe she was getting from their Mr. Miller.

He wasn't looking directly at the camera, instead staring just off to the side. His green eyes had a cut to them that said he was angry, or maybe, more aptly, annoyed. Carly could almost hear the sigh that had probably escaped his lips just after the picture was taken.

Or maybe she was wrong.

Maybe Noah Miller, former Amish, was trying for smoldering and overshot the mark.

Because, regardless of his intention with the standoffish pose, there was no denying he was a good-looking man.

And their first suspect.

Rihanna stood and collected her iPad. She was a straitlaced professional from tip to tail, but she'd spent enough time with the rest of them to be less formal when it was just the team. She nodded toward the picture.

"I already let him know that we might need his help and, let me tell you, he sounded as stubborn as he looks right there," she said. "He might be as forthcoming as a rock, but he agreed to at least meet us at the barn when we arrive."

They sat with that a moment, then the meeting was over.

The team filtered out, already making calls and preparations. Carly, who could have been among them, decided to stay seated. It was better to get what came next over with now rather than later. Alana must have agreed. She was quick. The moment the last of the team was out the door, she was hovering next to Carly, a look of pure concern on her face.

"A tough case," Alana opened with. "How do you feel about it?"

Carly felt the urge to sigh, right alongside the pain

that never went away. But, as she'd thought before, Alana Suzuki had thirty years under her belt with the FBI. During those thirty years she'd seen things that most never would. Not even the TCD team.

Discounting her concern was almost akin to discounting the trauma, pain and sorrow she had undoubtedly lived through.

So, Carly didn't.

Instead she finally looked down at her coffee and told the truth.

"To be honest, I don't know."

Alana put her hand on Carly's shoulder. A small moment that reminded Carly that she wasn't a kid anymore. She wasn't in that house. She wasn't in that kitchen.

No.

She was an agent with the FBI, an expert.

With a team who always had her back.

The same went doubly for their boss.

Carly felt the old fear inside of her harden into resolve.

Alana let go, realizing the change was happening.

When she met Alana's gaze, Carly was nothing but determined.

Justice wasn't just a word to her.

It was a promise.

One she was making to a stranger, someone who just didn't know it yet.

"What I *do* know is that whoever is behind this is in for a world of hurt," she said. "Because I'm coming for them and there's not a place on this green Earth where they can hide."

Chapter Two

Noah didn't know what he had expected next, but this wasn't it. He was standing outside of the community barn, hands deep in his jacket pockets and boots wet from the dusting of snow still on the ground, when the dark SUV appeared in the distance. It was followed by another SUV and a sleek black car.

Noah had spent the first sixteen years of his life seeing mostly horse-and-buggies along the main road in Potter's Creek. Even with buggy lights, it was a simpler existence. A way to stay closer to the world. Seeing the posh caravan go between open fields and modest buildings was a contrast Noah wasn't sure how to feel about now.

The group of Amish standing around the barn's doors weren't helping.

They were honest, humble men.

And they honestly and humbly did not like the idea of the Englishers invading their community with badges, guns and their own agenda.

Noah tried not to listen to his long-standing resentment as it reared its ugly head, reminding him that he was included in that group. At least as far as the out-sider aspect went. His father might have called him to the Yoder farm originally, but Noah was as welcome as the group of strangers from the federal government driving up now.

Nope. Not one bit.

The Amish of Potter's Creek didn't want him at all.

Which made the fact that he'd been asked to the meeting by the Tactical Crime Division's liaison even more awkward.

Noah hadn't been rude to her, but he also hadn't been kind at the request. He was all for helping in an emer-gency, but any other time he'd rather be on his farm, soaking up the scenery and tending to his cattle. Not an outcast, whose father and brother, no more than five steps away, wouldn't even look him in the eyes.

That is, unless it was to glare.

Though the glaring was left mostly to Isaiah Yo-der's oldest son, Isaac. The Amish might not be a vi-olent bunch, but Noah was sure if looks could kill, he'd already be a goner from Isaac's piercing gaze. And that was saying something considering Noah's younger brother, Thomas, was present. Thomas had been three when Noah left the community. Noah was sure his younger brother had heard over the interven-ing twelve years just how disappointing and sinful his older sibling was.

At least you're not dead in a field.

Noah shifted against the barn's worn wall as his inner voice reminded him that his personal issues rated low to nil at the moment.

Someone had targeted the community and that had ended in the death of a father and son, plus the loss of countless heads of cattle. Lives and livelihoods had been destroyed.

Just because Noah's own father could barely stand him didn't mean he couldn't feel the loss around them weighing on his chest.

Elmer and Stephen Graber hadn't deserved to die like that.

No one did.

"I don't like this," Noah's father said as the first SUV came to a stop just behind his truck. The barn behind them was almost exactly in the center of their community, equidistant from most of the farms. Yet all of the men had walked from their respective homes to meet, leaving their horse-and-buggies at home. Noah expected this was so their families had a means to get to them and their neighbors fast if something else happened.

"They are here to help, Samuel."

Their religious leader, Levi Raber, spoke the truth but there was a stiffness to his words. Noah didn't know the man well, but appreciated he was trying to keep the men around him in less hostile spirits.

Judging by the wave of tension that rolled over their group as the SUV unloaded its passengers in front of them, the bishop failed in his attempt.

It probably didn't help matters that the first person to approach was a woman wearing a tailored dark peacoat, high-heeled boots and lipstick that shone in contrast to her dark skin. She was tall and gave the immediate impression of being a professional. There was no hesitation as she strode over to the men.

"You must be Bishop Raber." She greeted Levi. Her confidence at whom she was speaking to was impressive. Noah recognized her voice as the woman whom he'd spoken to on the phone. "My name is Rihanna Clark," she continued, giving no room for a response. "I work as the liaison between the TCD team and local police, press and the public. Basically, I work at keeping everyone on the same page." She smiled and motioned to the barn behind them. "Thank you for allowing us to use your community barn for our headquarters. It will be extremely helpful to the team and the case."

Levi nodded, a curt movement.

"We were told you would need phone service. The man from the Center for Disease Control is inside using it now."

Rihanna swept her gaze across him, Noah's father and brother, and Isaac, smile holding strong.

"Great. I'll need to speak to him sooner rather than later. But first—" She turned toward the rest of her companions from the SUV. Noah watched as his father took each new member in with an impassive face.

He knew he wasn't much better.

Noah didn't have a distaste for outsiders like the rest of the community, but he wasn't enthused about an FBI team setting up camp so close to his home, either. He lived a private, solitary life. The sooner they did their job and put whoever was behind the attacks behind bars, the better. Then the community could heal after their losses, all while going back to ignoring him and his quiet life just outside of it. So he let his natural default of being the original outsider become his mask as Rihanna introduced her team.

Which was hard considering the first person up was not at all what Noah had expected when he had pictured the FBI.

"Let me introduce you to the Special Agent in Charge, Dr. Carly Welsh."

Noah struggled to hold tight to his unfazed expression. A feat, considering one of the most beautiful women he'd ever seen outstretched her hand at her introduction. She was smiling, but it wasn't friendly like the woman next to her. Instead, it almost seemed strained. Impatient, even. Like it was just one tedious thing to do before she could get right into the case.

She also didn't look like any doctor he'd ever seen. Then again, that was on him and his small-town living. There weren't many in circulation for a comparison.

"Nice to meet you," she said, adjusting the hood of her long, black coat. The blond hair that was trapped beneath it splayed out over her shoulders. It was on the shorter side, with a wave to it. Much more free than the tight smile across her lips.

Bishop Raber shook her hand and introductions were then given for the men around him. They didn't include Noah. Rihanna extended her introductions to the last passenger, but Noah didn't catch his name. Instead, Dr. Welsh turned her dark eyes directly on him.

There was no smile this time, tight or otherwise.

He stood straighter than before as she excused herself and walked over.

There was a confidence to her walk that gave Noah the distinct impression before she even said a word to him that Dr. Carly Welsh was a force to be reckoned with.

And she had her sights set on him.

PICTURES DIDN'T DO the man justice.

Not one itsy little bit.

Their link to the Amish was more than six feet of brooding masculinity and, in any other circumstance, Carly would have had to stop a moment and revel in how attracted she would have been to him.

But it wasn't as if she was with her adoptive parents, vacationing in Amish country.

She was here to catch a murderer. One with access to and the absolute nerve to use a deadly powder that had already taken several lives.

So Carly's brain put her body on lockdown the moment she saw the cowboy leaning against their headquarters.

She had a job to do, and that job included vetting their potential link to the community.

Though, judging by the berth the rest of the group was giving Noah, maybe Rihanna had misunderstood his significance.

In less than a minute of standing outside, Carly had already seen Isaac Yoder giving the farmer looks that could curdle butter.

It was interesting and concerning at the same time.

And absolutely the reason why she was about to take

tall, dark and brooding aside and flex her FBI muscles for a quick interrogation.

"You're Noah Miller."

She didn't phrase it as a question because they both knew that was exactly who he was. Since she'd already been warned that the farmer could be standoffish, she wasn't giving him an inch to wiggle. Though Carly did know that it was easier to catch flies with honey, so she at least made sure to keep her body language loose rather than ready to strike.

To his credit, he nodded.

"And you're Dr. Carly Welsh, from what I've just heard."

His voice was a low baritone. Not only did the man look intimidating, he sounded like it, too.

Thankfully, Carly had never been someone easily intimidated.

"That's me. Call me Carly."

He extended his hand, not something the men behind them had done, and gave the first smile she'd seen since they'd gotten off of the plane. It didn't last through their handshake.

"You can call me Noah."

He must have picked up on the fact that she was already in work mode so there was no point in dillydallying.

"So I hear that you don't want to work with us, Noah. I'm curious as to why you don't want help."

That did the trick. The man switched from stoic to tense.

"Like I told Ms. Clark on the phone, I don't think

I'm your best option for open communication with the community. I never said I *wouldn't* help. I just pointed out I don't think I'll *be* that much to you all."

Carly crossed her arms over her chest. The cold was no doubt turning her nose a bit red, but the jacket she'd had stashed in the back of her closet for half a year was right on the money for warmth.

"You're former Amish. Does that mean you were kicked out? Is that why you don't think you can help? Because you're an outsider, too?"

Noah didn't seem to like that line of questioning. Yet, he answered without hesitation.

"I chose to leave when I was sixteen," he said. "That decision isn't one many people around here understand or like."

Carly didn't know the man, but she'd bet every dime and nickel in her bank account that he was doing his best not to side-eye the group of men.

"Which can make communication more difficult, especially in trying times. I just don't think I'm the right guy for the job."

Carly took a small moment to consider the man. He'd *chosen* to leave. As she'd gone through her knowledge of anthrax on the plane, Axel had skimmed through Amish customs and beliefs. Some of them Carly had already known, others she'd been surprised by. Among the things she'd known about was the tradition of Rumspringa. It was a period of time where teens were allowed greater personal freedom and the ability to live outside and explore the world without Amish restrictions. After that time ended, they had to make the decision if they wanted to come back to the community or not.

What she didn't know was why Noah had been one of the few who had decided not to come back.

So she asked.

"Why did you leave? Don't you have family here?"

This time his frustration was immediate and aimed solely at her.

"That's extremely personal and, no offense, I don't have to be Amish anymore to distrust strangers." He squared his shoulders even more if it was possible, physically strengthening the wall that was him. An invisible barrier between her questions and his past.

Carly knew enough about those kinds of walls to dissuade herself from any attempt to climb the one that was Noah Miller.

She had no doubt she'd have better luck at convincing Bishop Raber to take a selfie with her. So, Carly doubled down on her conviction to get to the bottom of what was happening in Potter's Creek and dove right in to her bottom line.

"Yes. I'm a stranger and honestly, although I've spent time in St. Joseph County and picked up a thing or two in the last few years, I'm not familiar with Potter's Creek. Or you for that matter. So, no disrespect right back at you, but that's why I'm asking you these questions. I'm on a case and, from where I'm standing, you're in either one of two camps." She ticked off her index and middle fingers at each point. "You know something or did something that caused the death of human and cattle alike *or* you can help us figure out

who *else* knows something or did something that has
resulted in the death of human and cattle in this community. Anything less than either of those would be
wasting both of our time."

Carly put her hands back into her coat pockets and
noted, while it was warm within its folds, her breath
misted out in front of her when she spoke again.

"Since I know already that you have been seen tending your own farm not far from here around the times
the pastures would have had to be poisoned, I still have
to ask— Did you perpetrate this attack, Mr. Miller, or
know who did?" Noah shook his head. His jaw was
hard. He was gritting his teeth. Carly kept on. "And do
you have any interest in temporarily being a liaison for
us with the Amish community?"

This time he spoke.

It was low. One syllable filled with a lifetime of
something Carly didn't understand or have the patience
to get to the bottom of while standing there in Potter's
Creek, outside of their community barn.

"No."

Carly nodded, ignoring the ping of disappointment
that went off in her at his answer.

"Then I'll do us both a favor and stop wasting each
other's time," she said, making sure her finality rang
through just as true. "Goodbye, Mr. Miller."

And then Carly walked away.

Chapter Three

The doctor was kind and straightforward. His name was Carson and he was eager to help in any way that he could.

He was also tired.

Carly could spot that before she ever made it across the barn, and knew it to be true before he finished his recounting of what had happened on the Yoder and Graber farms.

Opaline had already done a quick workup of the man before they'd even left Traverse City. He was respected and good at what he did. Smart and skilled. But Carly knew better than most that there were some situations that got their hooks into you and didn't let up. At least, not for a while. It could beat a person down, make every part of them tired and ready for the madness to stop.

Carson might have been a good area doctor for Potter's Creek, but he was ready to go home. After Carly got the information she wanted, she obliged the man and watched him leave their temporary headquarters.

Then it was time for her to step up and call some more shots.

"Aria, Max," she started, pitching her voice so it was easier to hear in the spacious barn. Both agents snapped to attention, pausing whatever conversation they'd been having with Bishop Raber. Or, maybe *trying* to have. Aria looked frustrated. Though she did have a baby at home and had shown up to work more tired than not recently. The cold that had followed them into the barn probably wasn't helping her mood, either. They'd once joked about loading up the band and heading to Hawaii for a much-needed vacation where sunshine and warmth year-round was guaranteed.

"I need you two to go out and look for any evidence that the CDC or CSI might have missed. So far no one's found anything out of the ordinary, but it wouldn't hurt to check again. Start with the Graber farm and work your way back to the Yoder farm." Carly shifted her gaze to Selena, then Axel. They'd been in their own conversation and looked as enthused about it as Aria had. Selena was absently stroking Blanca's fur just behind her head, but there almost seemed to be some tension between her and Axel. Maybe everyone needed to get some more sleep.

"Selena and Axel, I need you two to focus on how the anthrax may have been purchased," Carly continued. "Use Opaline for whatever support you need. She's stationed at Headquarters until we say otherwise. As for Blanca, I don't want to pull her in until we have a clearer picture of what's going on."

There was no sense in sending her out into "the field" when that actually encompassed hundreds of acres of real fields and hundreds of people. Not to mention the possibility of that land being laced with more anthrax.

She'd rather have timid boots than brave snoots, as Selena often called Blanca's impeccable sense of smell, doing their first pass over.

"Aye aye, boss," Selena said. Her voice was tight. Axel glanced at her before nodding that he understood. Something strange definitely was going on between them but there was no time to dig into that now.

"Mitigation efforts have been ongoing and are almost over. But before everyone leaves, just as a precaution, I want you to have a designated pair of work shoes for when we're out in the fields," Carly continued. "Also, make sure you have at least one pair of gloves on you, keep your set of protective eyewear I brought with us in your vehicle, and if you have a cut or get one anywhere on you, then you immediately go to a first aid kit and disinfect and bandage. And, even though it should go without saying, if you come in contact with any powder, do not inhale or touch. Instead call Rihanna, who will be coordinating with the CDC, and then me. That sound good?" Her team nodded. "Rock on, everyone."

They started to leave but Selena caught Carly before she followed.

"What are you going to do?" she asked. "Perp duty?"

Carly nodded.

"They don't realize it now, but they've won themselves an all-expenses-paid vacation to Carly Island. All my time and energy is about to shift solely onto them."

"You're Carly Town and they're the only resident," Selena said. "And the mayor."

Carly gave her a friend a quick smile. They did this sometimes. Whistled in the dark. Took a moment or two to talk nonsense to lighten the mood. Smiled and laughed and said silly things to remind themselves that there was more in the world than senseless acts of violence and murder.

Whistling in the dark.

"I'm the only member in the audience of a one-man show and I'm ready to write a scathing review," Carly pitched.

"Before you were both marooned on an island, you were allowed to bring only one item each. They brought a weapon, you *are* the weapon," Selena gave back.

"They're up the creek without a paddle…because I have all the paddles."

"And you're not giving them back."

Carly snorted.

"No way, Jose. No paddles for our perp."

Selena's grin grew. She shook her head.

"We're so lame."

"But that doesn't mean we aren't professionals."

Selena conceded to that. Then her voice went low and any amusement disappeared. She leaned in a little. Blanca brushed against Carly's leg at the new closeness.

"Heads up, I don't think our Amish buddies care if we're professional or not," she said. "I overheard Aria trying to ask some questions and they went tight-lipped."

"But we're here to help them. By them not helping *us* they're only hurting themselves."

Selena shrugged.

"Just because we have badges doesn't mean they trust us. I think our best bet might really be that tall drink of water you were talking to before we came in. The farmer."

Carly felt her lips purse in response.

"And just because I don't think he had anything to do with the attacks doesn't mean I trust him to help."

"It's your call, boss." Selena gave Blanca an absent pat on the head before pulling her gloves from her pocket. "Just make sure you keep an eye out. Cell service sucks out here and if something happens we have a lot of ground to cover. Be safe."

Carly softened momentarily at that.

"You, too."

Selena and Blanca left the barn. Carly went to Rihanna to have a quick word, even as she mentally started listing the questions she'd ask the Amish men in her drive for more information.

Yet, when she turned around, the men were gone.

Carly swore beneath her breath and hurried out of the barn.

"Excuse me," she called out. The bishop was no longer with them, but the other three were in the process of talking to another man.

Noah.

Why hadn't he left already?

"Excuse me," she repeated, pushing through her curiosity and right into their group. She knew the men by their first names—Samuel, his son Thomas, and one of the victim's, Isaiah Yoder's, son Isaac—but past that they were strangers.

Just like she was an outsider.

Which, by how quickly they zipped their mouths shut because of her presence, *was* going to be a problem.

Still, Carly hoped that wouldn't be the case.

"Like my colleague said earlier, I'm the lead agent investigating what happened and need to get started immediately," she said in greeting, careful not to let her gaze stray over to the farmer. She focused instead on Yoder's son. He didn't yet have a beard, but there was a hardness to his eyes. One that settled when worry or fear refused to go away. "If you don't mind, I'll need a list of people who might want to harm the families whose farms were affected. Anyone who might want to hurt the community as a whole, too."

Where she expected an answer, Carly only got silence.

She felt her eyebrow pull up, waiting.

The men were all still, tight-lipped.

"Um, hello? Did you hear me?"

Then the Amish men did something she absolutely hadn't expected.

They turned away from her and started to walk off.

Every instinct in Carly's body was about to show those men the mistake they'd made, but Noah cleared his throat. Carly must have had heat in her eyes, because Noah held up one hand and gave a small sigh.

"Don't shoot the messenger, but they've decided all

questions and concerns you have should go through me if you want answers."

Carly rolled her eyes.

"Seriously? Is it because I'm a woman?" she asked. "Because you want to know what isn't sexist? *Anthrax*."

She might have imagined it but a smile looked like it was trying to pull up the corner of his lips.

"No, it's not because you're a woman," he said. "They're not sexist, just Amish."

Carly blew out a frustrated breath.

"And *I'm* just trying to help them."

"They don't trust 'Englishers.' It's just their way."

Noah joined her in watching the group walk away. Snow melted beneath her boots and the wind picked up enough that she had to fight a small shiver.

Usually Carly dealt with bad guys being a pain, not so much the victims.

"Listen, I can get you that list, but I'm warning you now that it'll be short." Carly heard the defeat in Noah's voice before she saw it in his expression. He didn't want to help, but he would.

"I thought you said that wouldn't work? For either you or them?"

The man kept his gaze on the retreating backs of the group.

"They might not like or understand me, but they've come to respect me over the last twelve years," he answered. "They'll answer my questions. You just need to tell me what to ask."

Carly held back a new surge of emotion at his words. It was as odd as the disappointment she'd felt at his earlier refusal to help. She still didn't have time to figure out what it was or why she was feeling it. Instead, she nodded to him and flashed what she hoped was an appreciative smile.

"The list is what I'll need first. Then I'd like a tour of the community, if that's something you can swing. They might be reluctant to finger a neighbor, but I need to know if anyone showed signs of murderous rage." They might have both been outsiders, but Carly was betting on the fact that Noah still had an ear to the ground of the community within Potter's Creek. At least way more than what she could probably get from other locals.

Noah didn't outright refuse, but he did check his watch.

"I can swing it but I suggest that's something we put on tomorrow's list of things to do." He motioned to the sky. "We've got maybe three hours left of sunlight, then this place gets as dark as the inside of a paper bag. I can still take you around, but you won't see much."

Carly actually smiled at that.

"Well we don't want to be stuck inside of a paper bag, now do we?" she asked, amused. "Tomorrow will be fine."

They exchanged numbers and he agreed to pick her up from the bed-and-breakfast they were staying at just outside of Potter's Creek the next morning. Now that he'd agreed to help, the tension had somewhat lessened in his shoulders, yet Carly could tell he was still ruminating about something in the back of his head.

And she found herself wanting to get to the bottom of it.

They said a quick goodbye, but Carly called out to him before he could get into his truck.

"Hey, Noah?"

The man paused. Then two forest green eyes were on her.

"Yeah?"

Carly closed the space between them and lowered her voice.

Despite her daily attempts to keep her past in the past, she knew what she said next only partially came from what was happening in the present. The rest?

A lesson she learned what felt like a lifetime ago.

"Don't let the belief that you know the people who live here cloud the fact that one of them very well could be responsible for what's happened. Knowing someone doesn't mean they aren't capable of violence, malicious intent or even murder. Sometimes the people closest to us are really only there to hide in our blind spots." She tried to give him a cheering smile to lighten what she had just said, but her heart wouldn't let her do it. The pain that hadn't left in over two decades was a constant reminder that there were some things so low that not even light could touch them. "We need to catch who did this and that starts with that list. Amish or not, someone here has to have an idea of who might be behind it, or at least a theory."

Noah took off his cowboy hat and thumped it against his chest, almost like he was saluting her.

Only a hard rumble that stirred something else within Carly.

"I'll do my best. You have my word."

ALMOST EXACTLY THREE hours later, the Tactical Crime Division team were standing at the fence line of one of the pastures on the Yoder farm. The sun was setting, promising darkness and a close to their first day on the case.

Their first day of more questions.

Their first day of no answers.

"We didn't find anything," had been Max's greeting when he and Aria had shown up. Now Max was leaning against the slightly warped wood of the fence and looking out at the trees in the distance.

Aria, who'd stepped aside to call her fiancé, joined him when she was through. Her slight frame often got her mistaken for a teenager in just the right light. It was one reason she fought so hard to be taken seriously. But everyone on TCD knew that she might have been small, but she was mighty. Now, though, she looked like they all felt—frustrated.

"If the CDC or CSI missed anything, whatever it was didn't have a shelf life long enough to still be around now," she said. "Everything has been cleaned up so well that you can't even tell anything happened."

Aria motioned to the pasture they were overlooking now. A worn red barn stood just behind them. The same red barn where Isaiah Yoder had been first examined by the doctor.

She was right, though. The light dusting of snow blanketed the ground, hiding any evidence that twenty-four cattle had died on the field less than two days before. And the beautiful scenery around the farm? It hadn't changed a lick.

It was still beautiful, breathtakingly so.

The air was cold and crisp and highlighted the contrast between the white snow and the evergreen trees. No traffic could be heard bustling by and there wasn't an ounce of light pollution. Just stars in wait, ready to shine.

It was a simple, natural beauty.

Which made the attack that much more of a slap to the senses.

"I don't understand why anyone would do this in general," Selena said, sidling up to Carly. She leaned against the fence and breathed out a sigh. "Never mind to a community whose whole spiel is about wanting to live closer to the land."

"Which makes whoever is behind this particularly malicious." Whatever tension there was between Selena and Axel was gone for the moment as he followed up to her point. He leaned against the fence, also taking in the same view. "They poisoned the land that this community cherishes," he said.

Carly shook her head, not to disagree but a small and futile attempt to distance herself from the present...and her past.

She rolled her shoulders back to try to move even farther away from the now-rising ache and tried to focus on the sunset.

A hush fell over the team around her.

TCD had become family to Carly in the last three years, but she couldn't guess at what they were individually thinking as they all stared out across the field.

It wasn't until the sun was down and darkness invaded the world around them that they packed into their vehicles and left Potter's Creek.

If they had known they were being watched, they might have gone much sooner.

Chapter Four

The Castle in the Trees Bed & Breakfast was, as one would guess, surrounded mostly by trees. Just outside of the Potter's Creek town limits, it was a shock against the evergreens with its light blue paint, bright white porch columns, faded dark roof that was partially steepled over the two-story parlor, and warm florescent lights, pouring from the windows to let everyone know that, while it was near Amish country, it wholly embraced electricity.

It also wholly embraced the Christmas spirit.

Wreaths with fake holly were pinned above every window and door while icicle lights hung about the railing along the wraparound porch. Three Christmas trees were situated around the first floor and, from the road leading up to the inn, two of those could be seen through the windows.

It was all very festive and merry.

The newcomers who had just gone inside were not.

Dressed in their winter coats and boots and badges and guns, they were not at all what Amish country warranted.

Not at all.

"I need you to keep an eye on them."

The voice belonged to a man who didn't have a badge, but he did have a gun. It was in the waistband of his pants, hidden by his coat, but the woman knew it was there. So did the young man next to her. They both had seen it the first time they'd met him and the few times he'd thought to remind them of it.

They all stood together some distance from the inn they were observing, far enough away that they could not be seen.

"While they're here and when they're in Potter's Creek," he continued, eyes like a hawk on the men and women disappearing into the inn. A woman hesitated and looked at the bicycle leaning against the front porch stairs. Then she turned her gaze out to the woods.

The man didn't flinch as she swept over their hiding spot past the tree line.

"That one," he said when the woman finally went inside. "That one might be trouble."

"They will all be trouble," the young man whispered. She reached out and touched his wrist to quiet him, but the older man already had decided he didn't like the note.

"They might be trained but they're out of their element here." He stroked his beard. Then he was smiling. He did that a lot. It never brought anything good with it.

"We stay ahead of them and we stay off their radar. And we do that by you two telling me everything you can about them and what they're doing. Got it?"

The bed-and-breakfast twinkled in the distance. The woman adjusted the strings on her bonnet. She nodded.

"Good," he said. Then that smile was back. "Because we all would really hate for you to break our deal, now wouldn't we?"

It wasn't a question for her to answer.

It was only another excuse for him to hear his own voice.

When he left them between the trees, she wanted so much to go home.

But he was right.

They had a deal.

One she would not break.

"You will search their rooms tomorrow while they are gone," she ordered the only other person in the world who knew why she wouldn't betray the other man.

He rubbed his bare chin, a habit he'd picked up in the last few years.

"And what will you do?" he asked, his voice so quiet the wind could have taken it without a fight.

"I will protect us." She stood up straight and felt darkness in her heart, as ugly hate replaced her profound guilt. "Even if it means hurting them."

NOAH MILLER WAS an early riser.

Carly should have expected as much. He owned and operated a farm with minimal staff to cover him when he was gone. He also had mostly grown up Amish, a lifestyle that required hard work. Unless he'd left the community to shirk a hard work ethic and an early rise-and-shine time, the limited information Carly had on him showed a man who had every reason to be punctual, erring on the side of early.

Yet when she looked up from her chair out on the inn's porch, one hand hovered over her notepad, the other around her coffee thermos, she still was surprised to see his truck coming up the drive.

Never mind the trickle of excitement that danced within her.

Noah was a mystery tucked inside another mystery and, for the life of her, Carly couldn't get past the urge to want to dig a little deeper. She *had* always been a curious creature. It was one reason why Alana had said she would make an excellent agent when the offer first came her way.

That and her extensive knowledge of biochemical weapons.

He put the truck in Park and exited the vehicle with a small, polite smile. Though there was nothing polite about the thoughts that joined her trickle of excitement at the sight of him.

His long dark coat was on but open, showing a red-and-black flannel button-up that was tucked into his dark jeans, cinched together by a belt with a silver buckle that shone. All items of clothing fit him and fit him *well*. It was by no means flashy compared to what Carly saw on the daily in Traverse City, but compared to the muted, no-frills clothing of the Amish, it made the man stand out.

It also didn't hurt that Noah was undeniably good-looking. Carly thought she might have overplayed his classic good looks from the day before but, as he approached the stairs of the front porch, she mentally confirmed she had, in fact, maybe underestimated their impact. Though, without his cowboy hat on, his long, tousled hair gave him the added appearance of being more rough-and-tumble than before.

It was a stimulating sight.

And 100 percent not the right time.

"Morning," Noah said. He shook the paper coffee cup in his hand a little and motioned to the thermos she was holding. "I came with a peace offering of coffee but I see you're already drinking."

Carly tucked her notepad into her jacket pocket and tried her best to continue to look normal. Most people didn't realize how often they were offered coffee, but Carly noted every time it happened to her. It was one reason she always traveled with one or two of her thermoses.

Carly Welsh always made her own coffee.

No exceptions.

"A peace offering?" she said in return. "Normally those come after you've done something that someone else won't like. What exactly have you done that I won't like?"

She gathered her phone and coffee and mentally went through her room upstairs to try to remember if she'd left behind anything she'd need or if she'd forgotten to lock the door. Her badge and gun were already secured on her belt and in the holster at her hip. When they were on a case, she rarely was caught outside of their accommodations without either.

"It's for me saying I wouldn't help yesterday," he

replied, as they walked to his vehicle. "You were only trying to do your job."

He went to the passenger side of his truck and opened the door for her. If Carly wasn't holding her coffee and her phone, she might have commented on the move. As it was, she accepted the courtesy and slid into the seat.

"But you ended up agreeing to help in the end. Which I appreciate, but I am curious why you did. You seemed pretty determined the first, and second, time you said no."

Noah sighed before closing her door and seemed to keep the sigh going until he was behind the wheel again. The cab of the truck was warm. He deposited the extra coffee in the cup holder next to his own.

"The way Isaac and the others were treating you rubbed me the wrong way. Then I realized I wasn't doing much better. Plus, I might live just outside of Potter's Creek, but the town is still my home. Someone starts attacking it like this and we all should be doing our part to help."

"Not to mention three farms have been targeted so far and you, too, happen to own a farm."

He nodded.

"There is that," he admitted. "I have more reasons to help rather than decide to mind my own business. Speaking of—" the engine came to life but he pulled a piece of paper out of the center console before reversing "—I did as much digging as my brand of shovel would allow yesterday and got the list you wanted."

A different kind of excitement started to get Carly's blood pumping.

The excitement of a lead.

Only two, by the looks of it.

"You warned me that it would be a short list," she said. "This is definitely a short list."

"And honestly it's more than I expected to get." He gave her a quick look. "You *do* have some knowledge about the Amish, right? They aren't exactly known for grudges, violence and driving people to murder."

"It's the people we never suspect of maliciousness that usually are the most capable of it. That's what makes the surprise that much worse." Carly felt her mood darken. "We can't write anyone off just because they seem like a good person."

Noah whistled.

"I thought it was innocent *until* proven guilty."

Carly rolled her eyes. She'd stepped into that one.

"In my line of work we're not here to sentence the bad guy, or even to put him on trial, we're here to *find* them. To stop the bad guys."

To make sure they don't hurt anyone ever again, she wanted to add.

But Carly could feel the cynical side starting to seep through her words. She didn't want to delve into the nitty-gritty of her past cases, or her life for that matter, so she was ready to let that thread of the convo lie.

However, Noah wasn't ready to let it go.

"I wouldn't call myself a natural optimist but, even to me, that sounds like a grim outlook to have for people. Do you really think whoever did this is from the Amish community?"

That was a question Carly and the rest of the TCD

had been repeating during their shared meal at the inn the night before…and a few times before everyone went to do their own tasks that morning. It was out of character for the culprit to be Amish but, then again, without more information they couldn't rule anyone out.

"I wouldn't be doing my job if I didn't pursue every potential lead," she said, careful with her words. "I can't count how many times I've heard people say they *thought* they knew someone after that same someone did something horrific."

"Like when you see friends, neighbors and coworkers during interviews about a shooter or serial killer."

Carly nodded.

"Exactly. Most people never see it coming. And only the lucky ones can wonder about it all later."

Out of her periphery she saw Noah shake his head.

"I just can't imagine someone from Potter's Creek killing. Especially with something like anthrax. They're humble and quiet as a whole."

"And Ted Bundy was a charming man," Carly hated to point out. "Monsters don't always look like monsters. Mostly they just look like normal people."

Noah let out another long sigh.

It gave Carly a few moments to readjust in her seat, trying to find a modicum of relief from the vise tightening in her chest.

Then it was time to focus on the paper in her hands. Not spout philosophy about good versus evil in modern society.

"So you have two people here that might want to do

harm to the community?" she asked. "Are their houses a part of the tour?"

He took the turn out of the inn's long drive and pointed toward Potter's Creek. Some snow stuck to the ground but it was balding in most places, showing sprouts of dark brown and green here and there. The cold was still around, but Carly figured without checking her phone for the temperature that it was a little warmer than the day before based solely on the fact that her nose was neither cold nor runny. Still, she had her black beanie tucked into her inner jacket pocket just in case her ears became too cold.

"Only one," Noah answered. "And he just so happens to be our first stop."

Chapter Five

The Zook homestead housed a family of six and, compared to the five farms that were in Potter's Creek, was small. That didn't take away from its appeal, though. The eldest Zook still living had watched his father build the simple cottage and, through time, had made additions to it to accommodate his growing family. That family now comprised Vernon and Sarah and their children Katie, Annie, Eli and Mervin.

Carly ran her thumb over the ink on the paper Noah had given her.

It was a small, subtle movement, but Noah couldn't help but appreciate the sight.

Carly was unlike any other woman he'd met so far, from her bite, her blatant skepticism and her pinpoint focus on the mystery she was trying to solve. She was keeping him on his toes less than twenty-four hours after appearing in Potter's Creek.

Which was why he was in Potter's Creek on a Tuesday morning, pulled over on the side of the road and staring at the house in the distance.

Because he sure would have been flat-footed and

on his farm right now if the FBI agent wasn't currently riding shotgun with a badge on her belt and a crinkle in her brow.

"So Eli is our person of interest," she surmised after Noah had given her a quick set of facts about the family.

Among their numbers and names, he'd also noted that they were one of the few families who had made a living in a trade rather than farming in Potter's Creek. Vernon Zook was a carpenter and had gone into business with a neighboring family five years prior. He was also one of the few Amish who had a separate shed structure out back that utilized electricity strictly for power tools, an uncommon but accepted practice given his vocation.

Noah nodded. He put on the truck's flashers and shifted to Park, cutting the engine. While Noah had gotten her the list and was her tour guide, he wasn't going to be a part of the equation when it was time to ask more pointed questions.

Right now Noah's only job was to drive her through Potter's Creek and call out facts about the Amish community. He wasn't eager to offer anything more.

Potter's Creek already had mixed feelings about him. It was probably better not to align himself completely with the investigating FBI. By the glares and stiff answers he'd gotten the day before while making the list, they were tolerating him but in no way appreciative of his presence.

The feeling's mutual, Potter's Creek.

"Yep. That's where you'll find Eli and his family," he said. "He's sixteen and, word is, has a temper."

"A temper?" Carly repeated, tilting her head a little to the side. "That's not uncommon for a teenager. Or for most adults. I personally have a temper when my caffeine runs low."

Noah could agree with that.

"*True* but apparently his temper ran a little too hot last month when Isaiah Yoder's daughter, Rebecca, also sixteen, wouldn't consider Eli for a courtship. Instead she started dating one of the Haas boys after turning him down."

Carly tilted her head to the other side in question. Her blond hair shifted at the movement, its waves softening her severe look just enough to make him wonder what she liked to do in her free time. Surely it wasn't riding with strangers with a gun strapped to her side.

"And since both the Yoder and Haas farms were affected, him being angry at getting rejected makes him a suspect?"

"I'm guessing you don't know much about how Amish courtship and marriage work," Noah said with a small snort. He was worried his dismissive tone would offend her, yet all she did was shake her head.

"Actually, I don't."

"Rule number one is that, if you're planning on being baptized and staying with the faith when you're older, you have to marry someone who plans to also stay in the faith. No one else."

"Okay so your dating pool is a little more high stakes," she guessed. "When you're turned down by someone, that dating pool shrinks without the hope of adding more to it?"

"That's the long and short of it. Not to mention it also doesn't help that everyone knows he was turned down and that now he'll have to spend years watching their courtship before being a part of the marriage portion that follows it."

This time Carly looked away from the window and at him, pulling his attention to her raised eyebrow. He noted freckles along her nose and the tops of her cheeks.

It was cute, a contrast to the gun he'd spotted at her hip when her jacket had shifted as she'd gotten into the truck.

"He'll have to spend *years* watching their courtship and then *participate* in their marriage?" she repeated. "Please give me some more depth with that one."

Noah stifled a laugh at her reaction. It had been a long while since Noah had been with someone who *didn't* know all of the Amish beliefs and customs.

"Every couple has the same steps they have to take if they wish to stay in the faith. It isn't a private thing. Intentions have to be made public and then your courtship *stays* public. If you want alone time with your sweetheart, then you spend that out on the front porch in plain view together talking. You spend it at singings. If you ride to and from church services, you do so in an open buggy and usually with a chaperone. Basically, everything you do as a couple is a public affair. *Then* the dance before marriage happens, usually around the age of twenty or so."

Noah had never experienced what he was about to explain, but he'd seen enough Amish engagements and marriages in his first sixteen years of life to be familiar.

"The first part is the same as it is for most English-ers. The young man asks his lady to marry him but then veers into a different path," he continued. "They keep their intentions a secret until around July or August, then the woman tells her family about her plans. Then the proper certification is requested after Fall commu-nion. Then all of the couples who plan to get married are 'published' at church. The deacon tells everyone the young women's names who plan to marry. *Then* the fathers announce the date and time of the wedding and invite all members of the church to attend. After they're published, the couple only have a few days before the ceremony and are allowed to go to one last singing with their old group of friends. After that the woman helps her mother prepare for the wedding while the groom-to-be extends personal invitations to all church mem-bers. Then the day of the actual ceremony, *everyone* gets involved. There's no maid of honor or best man roles. It's a lot of activity and not at all something you can easily ignore or just skip."

Carly returned her attention to the paper in her hand and Eli's name.

"Which means Eli wouldn't be able to avoid the fact that he was rejected by the Yoder girl for the Haas boy. He'd have a front-row seat of the entire thing, along with everyone else. Salt in the proverbial wound."

"Not an easy pill to swallow, especially for a rejected sixteen-year-old with anger issues."

Carly gave the house in the distance another long look before she pulled out her cell phone. Noah gave her privacy while she texted someone.

"Let's continue with the tour and then you can drop me off at the community barn," she said when she was done.

"Then you and your team will talk to Eli?"

She touched the second name on the list.

"Unless this David Lapp is more interesting."

Abram Lapp's eldest son had already popped into Noah's thoughts before the FBI had even shown up.

"What's that face?" Carly asked before he could reply.

"What do you mean?"

She touched the spot on her forehead between her eyebrows, then motioned to him.

"You scrunched up right there and looked like you just sucked on a lemon, all at once. I'm assuming that means you know David and he *is* more interesting than Eli."

Noah didn't want to, but he nodded to both assumptions.

"This is where my time outside of the community is going to show," he warned. "I don't know the whole story but I do know that David, nineteen now, left six months ago."

"Nineteen… So he didn't leave after his Rumspringa?"

He shook his head.

"He left after getting caught breaking church rules. Which is *interesting* considering he'd already come back from his Rumspringa with every intention of being baptized when he turned twenty."

Noah put emphasis on the word *interesting*.

"When you say he left, you really mean he got kicked out."

Now Carly was the one with a knitted brow.

"Bingo. And, before you ask, everyone went tight-lipped about what exactly he did to warrant being exiled." Noah snorted but he felt no amusement. "They might have a grudging respect for me around here but when you get down to the nuts and bolts of it, I'm still the *other* guy who left."

Carly was facing him again, but her contemplative expression had changed to something else.

Thoughtful? Sympathetic? Regret that her only resource didn't elicit enough trust from people who believed in honesty?

"Where is Lapp now?" she asked instead.

This time there was a snort of amusement from Noah. He turned the engine back on and checked over his shoulder to see if anyone was driving down the road. He didn't miss her look of surprise after he answered.

"Wouldn't you know it, he's actually my neighbor."

"Your neighbor?"

Noah nodded and pulled out onto the road since the coast was clear.

"I didn't even realize it until yesterday when I started asking around," he followed up. "I'd heard before then that David was still around Potter's Creek, but between working on my farm and not exactly having many reasons to be present in the community, I don't often get too much town news. Plus, I'd only ever met David once and that was in passing during his Rumspringa a few years back." Noah gave her a quick look. "It's not like I'm running some kind of post-Amish support group in my limited free time."

At that Carly chuckled. A nice sound that was equal parts pleasant and intriguing.

Settle down there, cowboy, Noah mentally chided himself. *You're here to help and then part ways. Not admire the FBI agent because she laughed at your joke.*

It didn't take long for them to get back to business after that.

The tour continued through the heart of the community and then by all of the businesses, farms and on to a few popular recreational spots for the town, for the Amish and tourists alike. Noah tried his best to give the facts with a few tidbits from the time he'd spent living in Potter's Creek.

Carly remained mostly quiet during the tour, asking him only to repeat family names and clarify a few details while she wrote notes. It wasn't until he was done giving his spiel on the abandoned barn at the back of the old Kellogg property that she made an observation of her own.

"You know, for a town this small, I expected every available space to be done up in some kind of Christmas decoration, but the only place I've seen anything is at the bed-and-breakfast we're staying in," she said, turning toward him in her seat, thoughtful. "Now I realize that that's probably another Amish-related thing I don't know and not just a town-wide disdain of all things jolly."

"The Amish celebrate the birth of baby Jesus in a strictly religious sense," Noah explained. "No decorations, no indoor trees, no *nonsense*."

He didn't mean to, but the last word came out sounding like a child mocking his parent.

Carly picked up on the change. Her eyebrow rose and she searched his face before her lips quirked up at the corner.

"And now that you're *former* Amish, you can go all out, right? Or do decked out Christmas trees and mistletoe not work with quiet-type farmers?"

Noah stifled a laugh at that. He hadn't been called a quiet-type farmer before.

"I actually have always loved the look of a decked-out tree—you know, the ones that look like a craft store exploded on it—but I usually keep it simple. A nod to my family, I suppose. Though, I'm sure if you ask my father, he probably assumes the inside of my farmhouse is filled to the brim with *all* things jolly."

Just like before, he hadn't meant his words to sour. Yet, they had.

Noah not only had a sparse Christmas tree, when he had spent most of his life wanting a grand, to-the-nines one, but he also spent the holiday alone looking at it. Something he'd told himself he had come to accept.

Still, there was a lonely bitterness there.

He could feel it like he could the year before.

So he handled it the same way he always had and tried to ignore it.

Noah switched gears and finished their tour. When

he pulled up to the community barn where some of the TCD team was waiting, he couldn't help but feel something else weasel its way to the surface.

A pang of disappointment.

It had been a long while since he'd had someone to share the beauty of town with.

And that wasn't for nothing.

"Thanks for all of this." Carly held her notepad up, eyes still tracing her notes. "I know Potter's Creek is small, but it's always easier to have a local to help fill in the blanks. Not to mention getting a lay of the land. It's not like Google Maps can tell us that—" she searched her notes for a piece of information "—no one uses the road behind the Kellogg property because the mud gets so bad buggies have lost wheels to it."

Noah nodded.

"It was no problem," he said. "I just hope it helps you all catch whoever is behind this. The people in town may be different from us but that doesn't mean they aren't good people."

Noah pictured two bodies in a field.

A father and son.

His fist tightened around the steering wheel until his knuckles went white.

When Carly spoke her words were surprisingly just as fierce as the anger he was feeling at the Grabers' murders.

"One way or the other, we're going to catch the person or people responsible and make them pay," she promised. "You have my word on that."

While Noah didn't know FBI Agent Carly Welsh well at all, in that moment, he found he completely believed her.

Chapter Six

The property's name had been changed to the Miller farm but the worn, wooden sign that hung out by the main gate by the road still read Tuckett Family.

Noah had owned it for upwards of five years and, in those five years, he hadn't thought to replace the sign once. The Tuckett family were good, solid people, those who'd passed on and those still here. Noah had spent his time running the place to the best of his abilities as a way to pay tribute to them, while the faded sign was a smaller token of remembrance.

Of respect.

Which was why his gut tightened when the first of his workers, a young man named Mark, took his hat off looking as guilty as sin and approached Noah after he returned from the tour he'd given.

"Hey there, boss," Mark said in greeting, his words drenched in what sounded awfully close to regret. "I heard about what happened at the Amish farms, terrible business, isn't it?"

Noah was only one step outside of his truck but he knew where this was going.

"Yeah, it is."

Mark nodded. His eyes went to the ground, then the pasture behind them, then finally back to Noah. He straightened, as if trying to prepare himself until he took a deep breath and went right to it.

"You know, I wouldn't normally do this, but the wife—well, you know she's pregnant with the twins and that in itself is already pretty risky and if there's even remotely a chance I could get them sick or infected, or worse… Well, I hate to do this, boss, but I think I need to give Potter's Creek a wide berth until everything gets sorted out."

There it was.

The first ripple effect of the attacks to touch the Miller farm, despite it not being targeted. Noah had guessed it would happen, but it still didn't feel good.

It also didn't help his anger.

Not at Mark, though. While Noah shouldered a lot of work on his own around the farm, there was a group of four to five workers who helped him. Mark was young, but had been at the farm for three years now and was as good and solid a worker as the Tucketts before him.

Now that good man was afraid that his wife and unborn children could be hurt.

And Noah couldn't fault him for that fear. He'd pick up work elsewhere pretty fast, given his good reputation.

"I don't think any of us will rest easy until whoever behind this is caught," Noah said. He clapped Mark on the back. "You go take care of your family. I'll be good here."

Mark apologized again, but didn't stay long past that. His truck wasn't even on the main road when another worker called in for her and her husband.

"I'm really sorry, Noah," Marjorie said through the phone. "We aren't saying this is forever, just until those suits can get a few days of detecting under their belts. Until then maybe you should think about taking a trip? You're welcome to come stay in our guest room if you need a place."

Noah accepted their decision but declined their offer. He didn't say it, but there was no way in hell he was leaving his farm behind. It was his home.

It was his place.

And there wasn't a soul on Earth who could move him from it.

He knew that his dedication, though, was his own and when another worker, Killian, called and recounted what he'd heard on the news and then asked if he could not come in, Noah decided it wasn't fair to expect or ask his last long-time worker to make the trip.

Regina Tuckett, however, wasn't like the rest.

She didn't answer her phone because she was already at the back of the property, wearing her snow boots despite the fact the ground was now wet, not frozen, and a look that was neither guilty nor apologetic when he walked up to her.

"This fence needs mending," she said, nodding toward the rotting wood that made up a small section between the posts. "I know it's still standing but it won't be for long. I'd rather we did it when the weather is cooperating, too. You know how I hate mending in the snow."

Noah laughed. He *did* know how much Gina hated mending in the snow because he'd heard her complain about it from when he was sixteen all the way up until the last winter at the age of thirty.

The main difference between him being sixteen and thirty was that Noah owned the farm now, not her father, and he never made her mend it alone.

"We can see about it next week," he said around a small laugh. "Until then, I think it's best you go home."

Gina turned on her heel so quick that her long silver braid slapped across her shoulder. Gina might have been in her early sixties but she hadn't moved slow a day in her life, at least not since Noah had known her. It was mostly due to good genes—all the Tucketts lived into their upper-nineties—but Noah wasn't about to discount Gina's sheer stubbornness playing a role in her ability to stay so spry.

She would dedicate her life to trying to nail jelly to a tree if someone told her she couldn't.

"Why on earth would I go home when there's work to be done here?" she asked, voice pitching higher than normal. "Did you suddenly hire someone else to help with maintenance and overseeing? Because, if you did, I'd like to meet them and see how they don't know a damned thing about—"

"—I didn't hire anyone new *or* replace you, Gee," Noah interrupted, holding up his hand to stop her from continuing her tirade. "Everyone else isn't coming in today because of what happened at the Yoder, Haas and

Graber farms. And I think it's a good idea. We don't know who decided to attack them and if they're targeting other farms. I'd rather none of you take that chance if something happens here."

Gina's eyebrow rose. Then she scoffed, surprising him.

"If you think I'm like everyone else then you don't know me, *boy*. There's work to be done here and there's no way I'm not going to do it because someone got their sick jollies off by preying on the defenseless." Gina motioned to her side. A shotgun Noah hadn't seen yet, but recognized as her father's, was propped up against her. "I'm not leaving this place until the work is finished and I dare anyone to tell me otherwise."

Noah took a moment to try to think of a persuasive argument but accepted defeat.

"I know from experience that reasoning with you is a loser's game," he said instead. "Just make sure you keep your eyes open and that gun down. Last thing we need is you shooting someone who just stopped by to snoop. Or, worse. Shoot an FBI agent."

No sooner than he said it did Noah think of Carly.

Gina's grumpy expression smoothed out and then dipped into curiosity.

"Is that why you came in late this morning?" she asked. "Were you helping them?"

Noah nodded.

"They needed a tour guide who didn't mind talking."

"Did you introduce them to your father?" Her words were genuinely curious. Gina had only met his father twice. In that time, it was apparent she wasn't too fond of him.

Then again, Gina was a Tuckett and they had never been known for being friendly, open books.

"No, it was just a point-and-give-a-brief-statement kind of tour. We didn't talk to anyone outside of the bishop when we ran into him next to the market."

Gina shook her head and turned back to the post.

"You shouldn't have to help fight for them," she breathed out hotly. "They sure didn't fight for you."

Noah knew Gina didn't intend for her words to wound, but they did.

"I'm not even sure I was all that helpful, to be honest," he said, sidestepping the reopening of the old wound. "It's not like I'm the most popular guy around town."

Gina waved a hand dismissively at him.

"Whatever you gave those suits was more than they would have gotten from the community on their own. Don't undersell yourself. If you think you're cheap then you're giving everyone else permission to think you're less-than, too." She took on a power stance, mindful to hold the shotgun with one hand so it didn't fall. "And what is it that Dad used to say about confidence?"

Noah could hear Frank Tuckett, standing in his work clothes next to the barn and wiping sweat from his brow onto his forearm.

"'Only you can make it and only you can break it.'"

Gina gave a quick nod.

"He wasn't a man who was in touch with sentiment, but he wasn't wrong."

Noah had to agree to that.

"I'll go look in the work shed to see if we have any extra posts still," he finally said after a companionable silence stretched between them. That was the Tuckett way, after all. Shared silence with bouts of work requests. "If we do I'll come find you and we can go ahead and mend this after I do my rounds. The ground's still not frozen, so we can handle it. Sound good?"

"Sounds good."

Noah started back for his truck, a chill in the air sliding into his jacket. The snow was gone but there was a forecast for rain coming up. He only hoped if it did snow, it wouldn't do it for long. He wouldn't deny that the farm and its almost one-hundred acres looked downright beautiful covered in white, but he also wasn't going to deny it was a pain in the backside to do his job when everything was covered.

Living in a scenery meant for a postcard was nice, but mending fences and other such chores with numb fingers was not.

Noah spent the next little while going about his duties, mostly maintenance since Gina had already seen to their livestock, before heading to the work shed in a hunt for extra posts. Painted a nice dark blue to make the worn wood look nicer, the shed was a small structure, half the size of the barn, near the back corner of the property. When Noah was eighteen he'd told Gina's father that the color had made the shed look like a piece of the night sky had fallen and gotten stuck in the trees. After ice had taken down a few of those trees that had once surrounded it, the rest had been cut and the fence had been built to include the shed in the field that went across one side of the property. Noah had also repainted the small building twice, keeping the same blue.

So now it was still a touch of the night sky, no longer *in* the forest. Just with a nice view of it.

Noah walked up to it with a smile, nostalgia moving through him like the chill in the air. He rounded the structure, trying to remember what all was inside before unlocking the door, but slowed in his tracks at the corner.

The shed's door was open.

Not unheard of considering the entire farm had access and anyone could be inside looking for supplies during a normal work day.

But today *wasn't* a normal work day due to the investigation and, apart from Gina, no other staff was on the farm. He doubted she'd been here or she'd have already looked for the fencing posts herself.

If that wasn't enough to raise suspicion in Noah, the blood on the wet ground in front of the opened door would have.

Without moving his gaze from the opening, he reached out and grabbed the only thing he could get his hands on as a weapon. The round-point shovel had a crack along its wooden handle but there was some heft to the tool. It would do in a pinch if needed. He flipped it upside down so one hand curved against the metal and the other around the wet wood. The muscles in his arms tightened. He moved to the door, careful with his footing so it didn't make a sound.

There were bloodstains, enough to notice but not enough indicating a substantial wound, he guessed.

If Noah hadn't been an observant person he would have missed the dark red spots, but there they were.

At his storage shed, at the back of his property.

During an investigation where farms in the community had been attacked.

Noah pushed his shoulders back and hardened his jaw.

Then, in one fluid movement, he rounded the corner, shovel held high.

It was empty.

Noah lowered his makeshift weapon after a quick glance around the room. Nothing was disturbed, though he could make out footprints that weren't his as if someone had been walking around.

They didn't stray far from the middle of the space and then they backtracked and went outside again.

Like someone had been looking for something but hadn't found it.

Noah managed to follow those footprints to the fence.

He stood there, a bad feeling starting up in his gut, and stared into the woods where they disappeared.

"What the hell?"

Chapter Seven

"I'm in a happy, healthy relationship with the love of my life, and even I can admit he's good-looking."

Aria was checking the safety on her service weapon. They were outside of David Lapp's house and readying to interview the boy as one of their two suspects. Axel and Selena had already gone off to handle talking to Eli Zook.

As for Noah?

Well, he certainly wasn't in the vehicle with them.

Which was great, considering Aria's subject change from how to approach the Lapp boy to how cute their former Amish liaison was.

Carly side-eyed Aria from the passenger's seat, eyebrow raised.

Aria gave a small shrug.

"What? I'm just saying. The farmer has that whole brooding, tall and dark-haired thing going on." She adopted a hilariously deep voice. "'I've seen things, Agent Welsh. That's why I brood.'"

Carly stifled a laugh, lest she encourage Aria to bring

Noah up again when Max was back in the vehicle. For now he was just outside on the phone with Axel.

"Calling other people brooders is like the kettle calling the pot black," she replied. "You've met our team, right? We all get quite broody from time to time."

"True," Aria admitted. Then she turned toward Carly and wiggled her eyebrows. "But I noticed that you didn't disagree that Noah is a looker."

Carly rolled her eyes.

No, she wasn't going to disagree.

But she wasn't going to encourage the woman, either.

Noah had been a good, well-tempered tour guide. One who had done what he could before delivering her back to her team.

Was his past mysterious?

Did she want to know more?

Was he really that good-looking?

Yes. To all three.

But again, there was a job to do, and right now that job had them parked outside of a two-story white house at the end of a pocked dirt road that had seen better days. A job that needed them to focus on the nineteen-year-old who had been exiled. Had not left of his own volition.

Max, thankfully, appeared at the driver's-side door before Carly could respond to Aria's teasing. He was frustrated.

"That was a short phone call," Carly said after the door was opened.

Max sighed.

"And, according to Axel, that was a short-lived interview. Apparently the Zook family were as forthcoming as a brick wall. A brick wall guarded by another, taller brick wall. The dad wouldn't let the boy answer any questions and that was as much as he said himself."

Carly grumbled but wasn't exactly surprised.

"I was hoping the cold shoulder we got yesterday would have warmed when they realized we're trying to help."

She got out of the car, moving her jacket back over her hip holster and the gun inside of it. Aria followed suit and soon all three were at the bottom of the porch stairs. Even though they were still talking, they each focused their individual attention on the house. There was a car parked at the side of the home but it looked like it hadn't been driven in a while. Since the house was by itself and not a part of a farm, it was the only structure in the middle of the open stretch of land around it. Trees could be seen in the distance. Carly wondered how far away Noah's property started but didn't voice her curiosity.

It would only get another teasing rise out of Aria.

Though Axel and Selena being stonewalled by the Zook family did give her a valid reason to talk about the man.

"If we don't get anywhere with David Lapp, I'm going to reach out to Noah Miller again and see if he's willing to help us. Better than us talking to ourselves and running around in circles," Carly said.

Both of the agents next to her nodded.

Without studying their body language, Carly knew they were reverting into full detective mode. Aria was noting every entrance and exit, Max was readying for the wild card option that inevitably happened during some of their cases.

Carly?

She had split her focus into two categories: on the lookout for dangerous toxins, and readying to do a verbal dance with David Lapp to see if he had been the one behind the attack using them.

"I'll lead."

Carly bounded the steps and rapped her knuckles against the front door. She had her badge up and out by the fourth knock. By the sixth one she called out Lapp's name, then her name, her affiliation and the need to ask a few questions. When that didn't cause any movement inside, she said it was time to split up.

"Check the perimeter to see if anyone is here. But be careful. Remember we don't know anything about this David kid other than he was asked to leave the community."

"Which is kind of a red flag," Aria added.

"Agreed."

Max went the length of the porch and then hung a left around the corner. Aria did the same on the right. Carly stayed on the porch but moved to the two windows next to the door. Both had curtains drawn.

She slipped her badge back into her pocket and kept going along the front to another set of windows. No curtains or blinds blocked the view of the room here. Instead, Carly could clearly make out a good-sized dining room with a table and four chairs. All five surfaces were filled with clutter.

Magazines, books, papers. Beer bottles. An ashtray with several butts on and around it. An empty vodka bottle. There were also a few paper plates with balled up paper towels. One had half of a pizza crust on it. Carly even saw a few dirty-looking socks strewn around.

Maybe David Lapp's general hygiene and cleaning habits had led to him being kicked out?

"Carly."

Max appeared next to her, his voice sharp, direct and low.

He'd found something.

"The bedroom on the back corner of the house has been trashed. Almost everything broken."

Carly pushed her jacket aside and unholstered her gun. Max already had his out, but low.

"Sounds like probable cause to take a look inside to me. Let's go."

They moved together to the back of the house, linking up with Aria. The back door wasn't locked so they wasted no time. In sync, the three of them raised their weapons.

Then they went into the house.

If a red flag hadn't already been waving in the wind before they entered, a trove of them were planted the second they were inside.

Stale.

Dirty.

Carly shared a look with Aria.

Max nodded toward the door nearest them.

Then it was time to clear the house.

They announced their presence a few times but were

met with silence. Still they moved, guns drawn, through the first floor. At the stairs, Aria walked up while Max went along the back part of the house. Carly wound up at the door to what she thought was a pantry next to the refrigerator.

But it wasn't a pantry.

It was a set of stairs to a basement.

Carly turned her head to the side, taking a quick breath.

A different smell wafted up at her.

She couldn't place it, but it didn't matter.

Something was way beyond not right.

Something was wrong.

She descended the stairs, her stomach tightening.

At first the room seemed normal enough. It opened up on either side of the stairs, making a big box. Her gaze lit on boxes covered in dust, cloths covering bulky furniture, a few knickknacks clustered together on different surfaces.

But by the time Carly walked off the last stair, everything about the basement, the house and David Lapp changed.

"What the hell?"

What was in the middle of the space to her right was so unexpected that Carly didn't see the man right away.

But she felt his knife.

Chapter Eight

The blood against her hand made Carly wish she'd kept her gloves on. It was oddly cold and concerned her a great deal. It meant that skin had been broken.

It meant that she was, in part, exposed.

It meant she was vulnerable.

It was the reason the gun she had been holding in the same hand had fallen from what was supposed to be a firm grip.

Carly internally swore.

The blood wasn't her only concern.

Maybe number four out of her five.

Her top priorities had already shifted three times in the last half hour since she'd been attacked in the basement and run after her assailant into the woods, Max coming up behind her when he'd heard her cry out. Aria had stayed to call for more help.

Now her priorities shifted again.

Find him.

Stop him.

Don't get killed.

Easy, right?

Carly swore again. This time it was from pain. A throbbing was starting to run across the right side of her face, while her lip stung to let her know without looking that it was probably busted where her attacker had socked her. Then there was the cut along her forearm.

The reason for the blood.

The reason why she had to catch the man who had done it all as soon as possible.

If he could attack a federal agent with such ferocity, there was no telling what he'd do to a hapless bystander who might have the bad fortune to be in the way.

Then again, Carly didn't expect to run into any wayward residents of Potter's Creek right now. Not several minutes deep into the woods. Which she believed was why her perp had hightailed it right into the trees when he'd first taken off.

Speeding through the dense trees and foliage would have been laborious under normal circumstances. Doing it in a pursuit was a downright pain.

A pain that Carly felt as deeply as the thumping of adrenaline trying to keep pace with her objective.

Her phone buzzed in her left hand.

She kept her pace but hit Accept.

"Where are you?" One of Max's underappreciated skills, in her opinion, was his ability to still manage complete sentences that were as clear as crystal even when he was out of breath.

Carly answered but she didn't possess the same skill. Her words were choppy and few.

She had been running for almost ten minutes under

the vast tree canopy, and the pain radiating in three different places across her body was becoming an obstacle.

"No idea. Before I lost visual he kept changing direction."

Movement rustled on the other side of the call. Max was somewhere in the forest with her but, what the Amish country might have lacked in modern technology, it absolutely more than made up for in expansive acreage and nature. The fact that she hadn't seen or heard Max since they entered the wooded area highlighted just how seemingly endless their current surroundings were.

"We might need to regroup," Max said as Carly continued deeper into the unknown. "At least fall back to me since you aren't armed. Aria's getting backup, but they won't know where we are."

Carly hated it, but she knew Max was right. She hadn't seen the man she was chasing in at least three minutes. Unlike Selena and Blanca, she wasn't a tracker. Her skills leaned toward toxins, biology and the mindset of someone who would use both as a weapon. She'd already started the ball rolling on an analysis of the anthrax used in the attacks. Samples were at some of the best labs in the country with trusted colleagues looking for clues.

Now she needed to use her observational talents to figure out why her attacker would have been in that basement and if he had been connected to the spread of the deadly bacteria.

But that's why you want to catch him so badly, her

inner voice reminded her. *Because what you saw in that house didn't make sense.*

Carly wanted answers.

She needed them.

"Carly," Max prodded. "Running blindly into a fight is a fast way for that fight to be a quick one. We'll find him."

He was right. Carly slowed her speed until she put her hand against a tree to catch her breath.

"If I'm not completely turned around, I think if I head east from where I am then I'll be out of here," she said after a moment. "Then we can—"

A branch snapped behind her and to the left. Carly dropped her phone, ducked and spun around just as a towering man with wide, dark eyes swung out with a closed fist.

The hit narrowly missed her but the man himself didn't.

Whether he meant to or not his momentum carried him like a linebacker right into Carly. She barely had time to put her hands up to brace herself against his chest.

Both went down to the ground.

All the air *whoosh*ed out of her as the man grunted at the impact.

Carly didn't have time to waste.

The man wasn't just bigger than her, he had the upper hand. One of those things she couldn't change, the other she absolutely had to.

In two fluid movements she brought her knees and

feet up and kicked up like a jackrabbit against his gut. Then used her hands to go for his face.

Her target was his eyes.

What she got instead was a few seconds of tangled limbs, grunts of struggle on both parts, and pain.

The force of her kick shifted him off of her but not before he pushed her hands away and angered her open wound on her forearm.

If she had had any breath left in her, she would have yelled at how it stung.

Instead she used the shift in the man's body to roll out from under him.

It was a move not without its consequences.

The man reached out and grabbed her jacket. Carly heard Max yelling out through the phone but all of her focus snapped back to her assailant the moment he used his new hold to start dragging her backward. Mud wet her face and chest. Pain from their first encounter in the basement merged with new pain.

Carly needed to end the fight now or it would be ended for her.

Using the same principle that had gotten her to the ground in the first place, Carly stopped trying to get away from the man and instead created her own momentum to use against him. She rolled back into him, knocking him flat against the ground until she was on top of him.

More pain shot through her as her knuckles hit his jaw.

Knocking him unconscious was her best bet.

Too bad she'd only brought her fists to a gun fight.

Her gun had slipped again from her hands when he'd come after her.

Carly threw herself to the side half a second before the man pulled a gun and shot. Her ears rang from the sharp crack cutting the air, but she'd managed to roll out of his aim.

As Carly scrambled to her feet, he pointed the gun at her again.

She didn't have time to be surprised that he didn't pull the trigger. He struggled to stand, weapon trained on her.

What had started with close combat had turned into two people six feet apart with a gun between them.

"You know, I—I didn't want to have to kill a federal agent," he said, not at all in a cruising calm tone. He sounded frantic, unsure. "But— but I'm not above it, either."

Carly raised her hands up, trying to make herself seem helpless. Which, given the lack of distance between them and the steady hand he was aiming with, wasn't too much of a stretch to believe.

"The penalty for shooting an agent is pretty steep. Don't be foolish now. Who are you?" she couldn't help but ask. "Because I'm pretty sure you aren't David Lapp."

Not only was he at least in his mid-thirties, the man had a shaved head, dark stubble across his face and, if the last half hour had proven anything, he was no stranger to violence. Sure, David had been exiled and was no longer a part of the Amish world, but doing such a hard one-eighty from that pacifist culture didn't seem to match the, admittedly, limited information they had on him.

The man motioned with the gun to turn around.

Carly's stomach tightened as she repeated the question and ignored the unspoken command.

"Who are you?"

That feeling of dread strengthened as the man smiled. Not an ounce of it was good.

"Wouldn't you like to know?"

He readjusted his aim to her head.

"I don't know what trouble you're in, but you're making it a hell of a lot worse. You don't need to do this," she tried.

"I know but it's easier than running." He wagged the gun at her again. "Turn around and get on your knees."

Carly had been here before. Well not *exactly* here, but in a situation where her life was a breath away from no longer being her life.

Being killed in the line of duty was always a possibility in what she did. Part of that truth was learning acceptance that a dangerous job could have a violent and unfortunate end.

But in that moment Carly didn't find even the hint of acceptance in her. There was no defeat, either.

Nope.

She was going to follow directions but try to keep him talking. Long enough for Max to show up. Or whatever backup Aria managed to get—if they could find them here in the forest.

And if she thought stalling wasn't going to work,

she was going to last-ditch effort her way backward into him.

Another tussle on the ground among the mud and blood.

Because Carly wasn't leaving Potter's Creak without finding justice for the livelihoods that had been destroyed. The lives that had been taken.

And for whatever had gone on in David Lapp's basement.

She had a job to do.

Dying in the woods in Amish country wasn't how she was going to meet her end.

Not if she could help it.

"Where is David Lapp?" she repeated as her knees settled into the ground. "If you're going to kill me then at least do me the courtesy of telling me that."

The man laughed, bitterness in the sound.

"I don't owe you anything, lady."

Carly didn't have time to worry that the man wasn't a talker. That he wasn't going to take her stall. That Max still wasn't there.

She also didn't have time to employ her Hail Mary attempt to disarm him or get away.

Or at least manage to take a bullet but miss a fatal hit.

The moment the last of the word *lady* left his mouth, a noise so loud and foreign that she didn't know how to react filled the morning air around her.

Carly put her hands down and whirled around.

Then, promptly, let her jaw fall open in surprise.

The man who had been about to kill her crumpled to the ground.

Next to him was another man.

Holding a shovel, blood now on the metal.

"Noah?"

Noah Miller was still holding his makeshift weapon like a baseball bat and breathing fast. His green eyes were wide and searching.

Searching her.

"Are you okay?" he asked in a rush.

Carly hurried to the fallen gun and scooped it up. She took a few steps back and trained its aim down on her attacker. When he didn't move a breath, she squatted down to check for a pulse. His body was completely slack, but it was there.

"I'm okay," she said, back to standing and still ready to shoot if needed.

"Are you sure?" Noah's tone dipped low. A quiet man until he wanted answers. "You're bleeding."

Carly was wet in places from mud, blood and sweat and she couldn't quite figure out which was which at this point. Plus, there was a pounding and stinging that accompanied several parts of her body.

But, all in all, she felt okay.

Nothing a shower, some soap and a glass of wine couldn't fix. Hell, maybe even a shot of whiskey. After her jaunt through the woods, she felt like she deserved it.

"I'm good."

Noah didn't seem to buy it. He looked so odd with his cowboy hat and weaponized shovel.

But he also looked so good. So, so good.

Whether that was because of his hardened jaw, the

unsaid promise that he was willing to fight again if he had to, or the sheer fact that he'd just saved her life, Carly didn't know.

His look of focus switched gears to a gaze Carly understood.

Now that the danger was over, he wanted answers.

"Who is he?" he asked. "And why are you out here? Someone from your team called my cell, asking if I knew where you could be."

Carly was trying to get her breathing back to normal. Her fatigue was starting to catch up with her. She motioned with her head to the direction she'd run from. Though she had no idea if that's where she'd actually started.

"We went to David Lapp's house to talk to him. He wasn't there but we found *him*." She looked to the man on the ground. "He attacked me and ran into the woods. Max and I pursued. Aria called for help." Carly stopped herself. "Wait. Why are *you* here? And with a shovel?"

Noah lowered his weapon but didn't put it down.

"I was getting something from my storage shed and saw some blood on the ground. I followed the trail to the tree line and then heard a gunshot." He nodded to his right. "My property line is about a hundred yards that way."

The way he said it, the way he looked—eyes wild with worry—touched her. He'd been concerned. About her. Carly couldn't help but give him a small smile.

"And so you ran toward the gunshot with a shovel?"

Noah shrugged.

"It's the only thing I had so I made it work."

She glanced back down at her attacker.

"You certainly did."

A rustling sound pulled their attention back toward his farm. Carly redirected her gaze. Out of her periphery, she saw Noah raise his shovel again. A few seconds later a woman with gray hair and a shotgun ran into view.

"Don't shoot!"

Noah dropped the shovel and put his hands out, taking two long strides to get between them.

"Carly, this is Gina. She works for me," he rushed to say. "Gina, this is Carly. She's one of the FBI agents."

The woman, Gina, didn't immediately lower her weapon.

"I heard a gunshot," she said, suspicion clear in her voice.

"It was him." Noah moved so she could see the man on the ground. Then she narrowed her eyes at Carly. "I'm okay, Gina," Noah added. "Put down the gun."

This time the woman listened. She didn't let it go, but she rested it against her leg.

"Federal agent, don't move!"

Another voice entered the area.

Max emerged, gun aimed.

Now Carly had to step in.

"They're good, Max! You can lower your weapon."

Max took a beat to look around, then listened.

Which was good considering Gina seemed ready to shoot them both.

For a moment no one spoke.

Carly took a deep breath and let it out.

It hurt.

She hurt.

But pain wasn't one of her problems right now.

What they'd found at David Lapp's house was.

Carly met Noah's gaze.

"Well, this might not be the time, but before we started a foot chase with this one here I was about to come find you."

Noah's brow slid up.

It only highlighted how attractive the man was no matter the emotion he was showing.

"Why?"

"Because we need your help." Carly let out another breath. "Because *I* need your help."

Now CARLY WAS back in the basement, absently massaging the bandage over the cut along her arm while drops of water soaked into the back of her shirt. All pain had reverted to a dull throb in the time it took for the local authorities to converge at the back of Noah's property to secure their alive, but unconscious, runner. EMS had shown up in the woods just as Carly's patience had petered out, but she'd sat there while they'd washed her cut, bandaged it and suggested she go to the hospital to get herself checked out.

Apparently she hadn't been a pleasant sight to look at.

Blood, mud and bruises.

Not the best combination to be sporting when you were trying to convince your team that you were fine.

Noah ended up being the only person out there who

kept his opinion on what she should and shouldn't do to himself. Yet, she'd seen how his gaze kept flitting over to her during their wait. Aside from that, he kept his conversation with his staff member, Gina Tuckett, quiet and private. The older woman still had her shotgun against her leg when Carly was okayed to leave.

She tried not to be ungrateful for the care—it wasn't their fault that the man had given her a good beating—but she had been nothing but anxious as each TCD member had gone back to the Lapp house to dig deeper.

Then it was just her, and she'd had eyes for only Noah.

The team needed his help.

She needed his help. More than the perfunctory aid he'd given so far.

However, before she'd even gotten a word off to try to persuade him, Noah had spoken first.

"What do you need me to do?"

Now he was standing next to her in the Lapp basement, clearly as shocked as the rest of them had been.

A chair was sitting up in the center of the space.

But it wasn't a normal chair.

Not at all.

This one was metal and bolted to the ground.

If that wasn't enough to be concerning, the thick blood-covered rope attached to it was.

And that was saying nothing of the dried stain on the concrete beneath the chair.

"What has David been up to?" Noah asked after taking the scene in. "Did *he* do this or was it done *to* him?"

Carly shook her head.

"Sadly, you're as up to speed as I am at the moment. When we first came in to clear the house I was barely a step off the stairs before Broad-Shoulders-and-no-Chill came at me. We're still trying to identify him." She motioned for Noah to follow her back to the first floor. "Can you tell me if you recognize or see anything that might have a connection to the community or why David was exiled? Or maybe where he might be?"

If he wasn't a victim.

"I can look but, again, I didn't know David even lived here until yesterday."

Carly passed him an extra pair of latex gloves and together they went to every room in the house. He was gentle the few times he moved or picked something up, much to Carly's appreciation, but was quiet through his entire search. It gave Carly time to build her own theory.

Something she shared when they met the rest of her team outside by the front steps.

"We are in the uncomfortable position of knowing almost nothing, but I think it's a good bet to think that David Lapp is either in trouble or up to absolutely no good. My gut says that it's the former and we need to find him ASAP." She nodded to Noah. "We're going to go talk to his family and depending on what they say, follow up with the Zook family, too. Selena, do you think you and Blanca could look around here? See if you can find something we've missed?"

"Can do." Selena thumbed back to the SUV she and Axel had been driving. "Blanca's asleep in the car right now."

"Good. Axel, stick to the house and see if you can't

try to build some kind of profile we can use to give us a better idea of who's been living here and what they might have been doing in the basement. I've already talked to Rihanna and she's going to let us know when she finds out who our Sleeping Beauty is and when he's ready to be questioned, whichever comes first."

This was the part that Carly didn't like about being the agent in charge—the uncertainty of whether or not she was making the right call. Especially given her limited information. But not doing anything could be a lot worse than doing the wrong thing sometimes and, when there was a deadly toxin at play, time was everything. So she trusted her first instinct with her last two team members.

"Until we have evidence, we can't assume the David Lapp angle, as strange as it is, is connected to the anthrax attacks. So Aria and Max, I need you to stay with our original case and keep looking into where it could be purchased and how it could be transported into the community without raising suspicion. That might get easier if we get some valuable info back from the labs I sent samples to or the folks at the CDC. But that takes time, and you can pursue other channels. I've already talked to Opaline and she's deep diving on several different angles with Alana's and Amanda's help." Carly took a small breath. The movement hurt the side of her face where she'd been sucker punched by the man twice her size. She didn't know what stung more, the fact that he'd surprised her or the busted lip he'd also caused. "Everyone good?"

The team nodded in unison, each expression turning

to pure focus on their tasks. There were no jokes any-more. No teasing or levity. Carly knew half of that was because of how bad she assumed she looked, while the other half was the image of the chair in the basement.

"Good. Everyone keep their phones on and stay alert."

They disbanded without another word.

Noah seemed to also be on the same wavelength. He walked ahead to his truck and had the passenger's-side door open for her before Carly was near it. He didn't say a word until they were headed down the drive to the main road.

"I don't want you to take this the wrong way but it might be easier to get the families talking if you... clean up a little."

Carly would have absolutely taken offense had it been any other situation, but she realized he was right. Her jacket might survive with a good washing and a strategic stitching at the arm but for now it was covered in mud.

Which might not have been all that bad had her face and hair not matched it.

Still, time wasn't on their side.

"The bed-and-breakfast is on the other side of town. I don't want to waste valuable time just so I can go wash my face."

"I was actually going to suggest my place. It's just down the road. And I promise no Gina with a shotgun this go around."

Carly couldn't help but feel a little thrill of intrigue pulling at her. She ignored it for the sensible call.

"If you don't mind, that would work for me."

Noah turned left on the road.

"I wouldn't have offered if I didn't want you to accept."

It was a normal, polite sentiment, yet Carly appreciated it more than she should have.

Chapter Nine

Carly was trying not to get blood or mud on Noah's hardwood. He could tell by the way she hesitated at the door between the screened-in porch and the kitchen.

"I run a farm," he reminded her. "You're not tracking in anything these floors haven't seen already."

Carly shook her head, then looked around to see if she'd shucked off anything at the movement.

"You saved my life today, *with a shovel*. The least I can do is be respectful of your flooring."

"There's a statement I never thought I'd hear. Or, I never thought to think about not hearing." Noah laughed and waved her in. "I got lucky is all. Now come in and don't worry about it."

She looked around herself one more time before admitting defeat, following him through the kitchen, great room and right into his bedroom.

"I don't usually have much company, so the guest bathroom is a bit bare at the moment." He opened the door to the en suite, his personal bathroom, glad that he cleaned it on a weekly basis. "There are towels in the closet just inside and you can snag any soap in there you like. If you want to give me your jacket while you clean up, I can work on making it look a little less like a Jackson Pollock painting."

Carly's eyebrow rose at that. He snorted.

"Surprised that a farmer like me knows art?"

"I'm not big on judging a book by its cover. That was just an unexpected comparison—" she looked down at said jacket "—but an apt one."

She winced as she took it off and handed it over.

Noah couldn't help but note the details after it was gone.

The ripped sleeve where she'd been cut by David Lapp's friend, *or* foe, had dried blood around it. The bandage beneath an eye-catching contrast to the crimson. The red and slight bruising along the side of her face. The dried cut above her lip.

The holstered gun she wasn't making any moves to distance herself from.

Why would she?

She'd already been attacked and come close to dying on Day Two in Potter's Creek. If Noah was her, he might even sleep with the gun beneath his pillow that night.

Just one of those details was enough to put fire into Noah's veins.

The same fire that had flamed to life the moment he'd seen the man aiming a gun at Carly.

The same fire that threatened to burn through his resolve to stay quiet while the TCD team and local authorities worked the scene.

The same fire that had seared into him the absolute need to do anything and everything to help the agents.

To help Carly.

Even though it was clear the woman could handle herself.

"I'll be in the kitchen," Noah said, trying to remain impassive. "Yell if you need me."

"Will do."

Carly disappeared into his bathroom and Noah retreated to the kitchen, all the while replaying what had happened in the woods over and over in his head.

Violence wasn't a new concept to him, but seeing it so close to the community he'd grown up in? It was different than the attack on the farms. That had been deadly, but silent.

The man in the woods had been a loud, physical assault. Not something to overlook until it was too late.

What in the world was going on in Potter's Creek?

It was a question that added to the loop of thoughts running through his head as he tried to clean up the agent's jacket. By the time Carly emerged from the bathroom, it was his turn to admit defeat. He'd gotten the mud off, but it had seen better days, that was for sure.

The same could have been said for Carly, objectively speaking. Noah hadn't known her before yesterday, but he bet it was safe to say she didn't always have cuts and bruises on her. Yet, even with her hair slicked back, her face void of makeup, highlighting the marks along her face, there was a natural beauty to her.

A beautiful simplicity.

A glow.

She smoothed down her blouse and seemed, for a moment, uncomfortable.

But then she smiled.

It was small and unexpected.

"I guess I should have listened to Selena and packed a second jacket, just in case." She looked at her long, dark jacket spread out on the countertop. "Even from here it looks a bit rough."

"It just needs some time to dry, I think, *but* I did go ahead and grab this out of the spare room if you want to borrow it." Noah held out a coat. It was long and chestnut brown. "Beckett only ever wore it twice, so it's basically brand new."

Carly took it with another eyebrow raise. Noah could smell his bodywash wafting off of her. It felt oddly intimate.

"Beckett? I didn't realize you were married."

Noah tried not to laugh at that.

"Beckett is Gina's little sister. Their family owned this farm before I did. On the rare occasion Beckett comes to visit Gina, she stays in the guest bedroom since it used to be hers."

She slid the coat on. It was a good fit.

"Wow. That's pretty generous of you," she said. "I once met the man who rented my apartment before I did and promptly changed the locks."

Noah chuckled.

"I didn't just get the farm from the Tuckett family. I started living here when I was sixteen."

That clearly surprised Carly.

She wasn't the only one.

Gina's parents agreeing to let him stay on the farm to work for room and board when he was sixteen had caused several waves of gossip. The fact that he'd remained had caused even more.

When he'd taken ownership of the farm?

He'd felt like a gameshow contestant with the locals asking him all the same questions: Why not Gina or her sister, Beckett?

Noah never answered, partly because it wasn't their business.

And partly because he wasn't sure himself.

"So Gina is like family then," Carly guessed, surprising him that she hadn't gone for any of the normal questions. Her expression was thoughtful.

Curious, yet respectful.

It was a nice change of pace from what he was used to hearing around Potter's Creek when it came to his past.

"I wouldn't say family—Gina would be the first to tell you she's not big into people—but she is a friend."

"And an employee, too?"

He nodded.

"After I took over the farm she only asked two things of me—to give her a job maintaining this place until she was ready to retire and let Beckett stay in the main house when she visited so they didn't kill each other." Noah shrugged. "Both requirements benefit me seeing as Gina is a loyal, hard worker and when those two are stuck together in the same place for too long the yelling starts." He grimaced at the memory. "And boy, those two can get loud."

Carly snorted.

"Being cooped up can do that to some people."

She pulled her phone from her pocket and frowned at its screen. Noah took the time to grab his thermos from the counter, glad for the umpteenth time that it worked its magic by keeping his coffee warm.

Carly let out a sigh, as he appreciated the warmth after taking a long pull.

"Opaline, our tech guru, is having a hard time finding anything on David Lapp." Her fingers flew across her phone's keyboard, brow creasing. "I was hoping he would have some social media accounts we could use to find him..."

Noah watched as she mouthed what she must have been typing, her frustration clear in how her shoulders tensed.

Was this how her every day looked? How her cases played out?

Their Tactical Crime Division name certainly didn't sound like they were dispatched to normal, run-of-the-mill issues.

"All right, I'm ready," Carly said with a nod to herself. She slipped her phone in Beckett's coat pocket and looked to him with a polite, yet small, smile.

That smile went away in a flash as her eyes went to his thermos.

Noah didn't understand the change.

"Do you want me to make you some?" He motioned to the coffee maker.

Carly shook her head, but her gaze stuck to his drink.

Then she brought out another small smile.

But something had changed.

"Washing my face woke me up." Her tone was flat. Noah didn't have a chance to question it. She was out of the house in a flash.

Noah realized it was about time he added Carly Welsh to his list of mysteries currently playing out in Potter's Creek.

DAVID LAPP'S FATHER said his son wasn't home with such deep disapproval that Carly believed him on the spot. There was no way he would be hiding David on his property. That much was clear, even to an outsider like her.

And that was before she had even broached the reason why they were really there to talk to him.

"The house that David is currently renting has a chair in the basement. A chair that's *bolted* to the ground and has restraints attached to it. We believe it was used to hold someone against their will."

As Carly spoke, the patriarch's face registered two things at once.

Surprise. Disgust.

She knew before she asked that this was all news to him.

Still, Carly had to do her job.

"Do you know why that chair is down there?"

Abram Lapp shook his head so firmly that his beard trembled at the movement.

"No," he said quickly. "I have never even been to that house."

It was the first time since they'd stepped onto the

Lapp home's front porch that the man had addressed her directly and not Noah.

Shock usually did that to people. They forgot to guard themselves.

"There was also a man who fled from the house," she continued, pulling up the picture of her attacker on her phone. "Do you recognize him?"

Abram pushed his glasses up his nose and leaned forward slightly. He was hesitant to look at the picture but, based on what she'd just told him, there was no doubt a curiosity there, despite him not trusting her.

"I do not," he said after squinting at the image. "Who is he?"

Carly returned the phone to her pocket.

"That's what we're trying to figure out."

Abram seemed to remember whom he was talking to and reverted his attention to Noah.

"Do you think David had something to do with this chair and man?"

Noah let out a sigh.

"I don't know a thing about him, other than both the chair and the man were in his house and that you're his father." Noah paused. "And that he'd been kicked out of the community. That's why we're here. We're asking *you* if you think David had something to do with it."

Abram Lapp took a great offense to that, though Carly couldn't tell which part had creased his brow and made his nostrils flare.

Noah's body language changed in tandem.

He'd noticed the anger before it spewed out of Abram's mouth.

"If you had asked me a year ago about David, I would have been happy to tell you that he was abiding by our teachings and well on his way to being baptized."

"But now?" Carly interjected.

It earned her a stiff look.

"Now he's living a life separate from ours. I could no more tell you if he was in the city on the streets than I could tell you if he was walking on the moon. Since he left the community, he left us."

"But he didn't *just leave.* The church decided to kick him out," Noah said. His voice had stiffened considerably. "That's not something that happens lightly around here, especially for people who want to be baptized."

Abram opened his mouth to say something but then caught himself. Carly used the opening to apply more pressure.

"If David wasn't the one keeping someone in that chair then it's very possible he himself was being kept *against his will* in that chair. You can be mad and frustrated all you want at your son, but I have to believe, whether on the city streets or the moon, you'd still care if something bad happened to him." Abram met her gaze but made no show of wanting to respond.

So Noah brought it home.

"Abram, the TCD team is here because someone brought violence and death to the community and values you have sworn to uphold and protect." He reached out and put a large hand on Carly's shoulder. Warmth radiated from his touch.

He was humanizing her to Abram with physical contact.

And it felt nice. She didn't pull away.

"Agent Welsh is only here to see that whoever is doing this is caught and held accountable, so Potter's Creek can go back to normal. So that the rest of your family doesn't have to be afraid to tend their own crops and walk their own fields. So, please, answer her questions or I'll have to go talk to Dad—" he lowered his voice "—and none of us want that."

Noah squeezed Carly's shoulder. If she hadn't been so hyperaware of it already, it might have thrown her off her game.

"We need to know why David was asked to leave here," she said, getting to the bottom line.

Abram took a second.

Then caved. He ran his thumbs beneath his suspenders.

"He violated the Ordnung," he started, dropping his voice lower. "He lied to us, stole from us and was caught sneaking out several times."

Carly raised her eyebrow at that.

"Why?"

Abram shook his head.

"Abram," Noah prodded. "What did I just—"

"He wouldn't tell us," he interrupted. "Even when being exiled was threatened, he refused to explain himself."

The man took a step back, closer to the front door. A woman could be seen through the window but she made no show to come outside.

"That is all I have to say." Abram looked to Noah. "To any of you."

He retreated into the house, leaving Noah and Carly

to themselves, and nowhere closer to answering any of their questions.

It made Carly's resolve not to show her frustration crack when they were back in the truck.

"We tell him his son could be in danger or be *part* of the danger, and he gives us almost nothing to work with?" She felt a growl in her chest but was still trying to seem professional. It didn't work. She turned to face the man who had gone stoic next to her. "Is that how your father talks to you?"

She hadn't meant the last question to come out, but there it was.

This case had to be hitting on some kind of nerve for Noah, right?

He turned the engine over.

"You're assuming we talk. Until this, we didn't."

Carly had no reason to feel defensive of the man next to her, but she did.

"The Amish are all about making your own choices, right? That's why you aren't baptized until you're an adult. So if you choose not to, aren't they supposed to respect that?" she asked. "Is it really that bad to be an outsider?"

They might have been good at playing off one another to get Abram to open up the little he had, but now Carly felt the off-limits part of Noah Miller activating.

"You'd have to ask them that. Not me." Invisible walls sprung into place between them. His words had a finality to them. An *I'm not going to talk about it* in fine print.

Carly pressed on, unable to stop the line of questions queuing in her mind.

"Is that why *you* left? Did you already have problems with your dad and the others and wanted to get away from them?"

Noah put the truck in Reverse. He was as tense as she'd seen him since they met. This wasn't his usual quiet or brooding nature. No charming little smile graced his lips.

He had shut down right before her eyes.

"Why I left has nothing to do with the case now, so there's no reason to talk about it."

And so he didn't.

Not a word.

Not a peep.

Chapter Ten

When Carly stepped into the inn kitchen late that night to grab a quick meal, she was surprised to discover Rihanna had beat her to it.

"I'm not used to seeing you up this late," Carly said with a smile. Rihanna was still in her business pantsuit, though she'd replaced her heels with worn plaid slippers.

"And I'm not used to being one of the last ones up," she returned with her own smile. It was tired and led right into the heart of the matter. "What I *am* used to is feeling like I'm being pulled every which way on a case—that's the entire job of being a liaison after all, trying to bridge together two sides—but *this* case…" Her brow scrunched as she looked down at her empty plate. She was trying to find the right words. After a moment, she sighed and shook her head. "It just feels like there's a lot going on and I can't track half of it, which makes bridge building a very literal shot in the dark. And I don't like that at all."

Carly knew the feeling. She said as much, but then tried to be comforting. Or, at least, somewhat so.

"The great thing about the TCD is it isn't a one-man

show. It's essentially a think tank with combat training, years of individual experience and one adorable dog. At the end of the day, it's not just us out there looking for answers. It's a team of people who want to see the bad guys caught and get justice." Carly patted her friend on the shoulder and then moved to the freezer to get her food. "That's all to say that this case might feel like a bunch of puzzle pieces, moving all over the place but we're moving pieces, too. We'll put it together. Soon." Carly smiled again and tried to lighten the mood with a shrug. "Or we won't. But then we'll just fail together, too, and isn't there some comfort to be had in that?"

That did it.

Rihanna raised her fist in the air with a mock cry of, "Go team!" The tension within her seemed to lessen all at once. Then she just looked tired. She waited until Carly was done preparing her noodles and walked her to the stairs, bringing a yawn along with her.

"You know, during all of this there's one person whose name keeps popping up on all sides."

"Noah," Carly guessed.

Rihanna nodded.

"Do you trust him?"

Carly was caught off guard by the question but, even more, by her answer.

"I think he's trying to help when there's no gain in it for him. And I don't think that's something we're used to seeing all that much."

Rihanna agreed to that, but before she left the stairs she paused. Carly followed what she said with a question. "Do you? Trust Noah?"

Rihanna considered that a moment. What she decided on hadn't been what Carly had expected, either.

"I don't have a lot of information on him and that makes me nervous."

They both said good-night, and Carly made her way to her room, still unsettled and restless.

She took off the robe she'd thrown on to go to the kitchen and sat cross-legged in her T-shirt and underwear on the bed, with microwaveable noodles in her hand and thoughts of a certain farmer in her head.

It was almost midnight and, as far as she could tell, she was probably the only one still awake. Or, at least, moving around. She'd heard Selena take Blanca out in the yard an hour before, but then both had gone quiet in the next room. Axel, a pacer by nature when it came to a particularly hard case, had worn the carpet out along their hallway for a half hour in thought. If he was pacing now, it was in the quiet of his room. As for Max and Aria, Carly had heard them talking next to the bathrooms, something about their kids, an hour or so before, but now both parents were behind closed doors.

Carly poked at the plastic container with a fork. She let her thoughts wander, but they were coming back to a very specific path.

A path they had been exploring since her first moment seeing Noah in Potter's Creek. A path she had no time to travel, yet there she was.

Thinking about Noah Miller and wondering if she really did trust him.

He had good intentions, but good intentions were

just actions not yet taken. They weren't worth much and could change as swiftly as the weather.

They also didn't equal trust. But there was just something about Noah. He'd come to her rescue. He'd been genuinely concerned for her, even worried.

She didn't *not* trust him. That would have to be enough for now.

Her eyes unfocused as her thoughts shifted.

Despite all of their discoveries that day, no one had any new answers. Her own contacts hadn't yet traced this strain of anthrax to a particular lab or vendor, but more testing might yield better results. Axel had spent the remainder of the day in David Lapp's house, trying to piece together a profile, but had come up short. He wanted another crack at it in the morning. Selena and Blanca hadn't found anything new, either, and would be turning back to transportation angles of how the anthrax came to Potter's Creek. Aria and Max were also trying to figure out where one might get that much anthrax and said they had a lead to follow first thing the next day. Opaline was also still doing her internet thing, while Alana said she was reaching out to some of her contacts in Washington for more information that might help them.

Everyone was *working*, yet there she was in her underwear at a bed-and-breakfast, with no real progress.

She hated it.

Every day, every moment counted, and she felt like she was wasting precious time running down information that was leading nowhere faster than they were leading somewhere.

Carly didn't realize her gaze had drifted over to her empty coffee mug across the room until a familiar ache thumped in her chest.

Button it up, Welsh, she thought. *Let's go back to thinking about the farmer and how he'd made a shovel sexy.*

It was a self-imposed distraction, but it did the job.

Carly imagined the man sitting next to her, his deep voice intriguing not only her mind but her body, and repeating his earlier suspicions before he'd dropped her off at the inn.

"Nothing ever happens here in Potter's Creek, and now? Biological weapons, a missing boy who happens to be a suspect in the attack and an unknown man found hidden in his basement along with a chair that couldn't have been used for anything good? That can't be a co-incidence. They have to be connected, right?"

It certainly felt like they were.

But who had poisoned the fields?

Who was keeping whom in that basement?

Why couldn't they find anything on the man who had attacked her yet?

And where was David Lapp?

Carly looped a noodle around her fork's prongs.

Connected or not, him being right or wrong didn't matter. Noah stayed in her thoughts as she finished eating, brushed her teeth and eventually crawled beneath the bed sheets.

Whatever the next day might bring, she found herself looking forward to seeing him again.

Invisible walls and all.

THE AGENT TURNED off the light at fifteen minutes past one. Darkness filled the room. It triggered the camera's night-vision mode. Suddenly the small bedroom was shades of gray, green and black.

He watched as Agent Welsh turned onto her side, her hair shifting over the pillow behind her. Her phone was on the nightstand, a light flashing as it charged.

She had no idea she was being watched.

Which was good, considering this was his Plan B.

"It's not right to watch a woman like that," said the boy next to him. He was dreadfully annoying. His mother, even more so.

She wasn't with them now, but he had no doubt she would have something to say tomorrow when the boy told her. Or maybe she'd just give him that judgmental look she was so good at.

She might not have approved of him or his methods to get what he wanted, but he had enough leverage on her so that it didn't matter what she approved of or liked.

She had to follow his instructions.

Or face the consequences they both knew she wasn't willing to face.

"I wouldn't have needed you to put the camera in if you'd done your job in the first place," he reminded the boy. "This is your fault, not mine."

The boy went quiet, a pout pushing out his lip.

"You're going to sit here until she wakes up and then tell me everything she does or says relating to the case," he continued. "Any phone calls she makes or any visitors she has. If you see her writing anything down or anything else of interest, then we'll just have to send our secret weapon in there to get whatever it is. Got it?"

The boy nodded.

"Good." He stood and stretched. He wanted a beer or some whiskey. Though he'd take some vodka if it was offered. He pulled his coat off of the back of the chair and slipped it on, the keys in his pocket rattling at the movement. When he was all situated he motioned to the bank of other monitors around the room. Five more screens showed sleeping people in shades of green, gray and black.

"The same goes for the rest of the agents."

RODNEY LEE HAD a rap sheet that was as long as his anger was deep when he finally woke up in the hospital. Opaline got a hit on his identity around the same time he managed to knock out an orderly and put the deputy guarding his room into the ICU.

Carly got the first call while she was riding in silence with Noah. It was almost ten in the morning, and they'd just left the interview with Eli Zook and his father.

Eli might have been an angry, angsty teen but as far as Carly was concerned that's where it began and ended. Unless they found evidence to the contrary, Carly took him off their list of suspects.

"He has one count of grand theft auto, a slew of misdemeanors for drug possession and a few disorderly conducts with one drunken disorderly…" Opaline's words trailed off. Carly could hear fingers clicking across the keys on a keyboard. "The last of the charges was three years ago in Detroit. After that he disappeared."

"Disappeared?" Carly repeated. "How so?"

"The trail for him goes cold a day after he was released from the police department after spending the night in the drunk tank. He was supposed to report for a hearing a month later but didn't. According to his landlord at the time, one day he was there and the next all of his stuff was gone with no forwarding information. He even left his car in the parking garage."

"And no one reported him missing?"

There was movement on the other side of the call. Carly could imagine Opaline's pink-tipped hair nodding along with her head.

"His grandmother filed a missing persons report a week after he was released, but the detective who was working the case concluded that Lee had taken off of his own volition. He didn't figure out where that was or why."

"And there's no connection or reason you can see that Lee would be here in Potter's Creek?"

"Not so far. His grandmother is his only listed relative and the people he used to pull stunts with are still local to Detroit."

Carly took in a deep breath of frustration.

The scent of trees and spice almost made her stumble in her response—was Noah wearing cologne?—but she caught herself.

"We need more information. David Lapp is our lead suspect right now, and it can't be coincidence that a man like Lee is just chilling in his basement, waiting to attack federal agents. When he wakes up, we'll have to see if we can't get more."

The second call came as Carly asked Noah to drop her off at the community barn. Since she'd pried into his past with his father the day before, he'd gone quiet on her. Only spoken when she prompted him or if the interview called for it.

Carly decided she didn't like not talking to him, even if it was just about the case.

So much so that she was about to ask if she could treat him to some lunch for all of his help when her phone started to ring.

This time it was Rihanna.

Her words were clipped.

"Carly, Rodney Lee escaped."

That changed the rest of Carly's day on the spot. Noah, who must have heard Rihanna, kept on to the community barn but sat quiet as she made call after call. When she was finally off of the phone, lined with enough tension to give a taut rubber band a run for its money, she did one thing that normally she never would.

Carly leaned her head back against the seat and closed her eyes.

Then Noah put his hand on her shoulder, like he had standing on the Lapp front porch.

Carly opened her eyes, startled, but met his gaze.

"We'll figure it out," he said, all baritone. "I promise."

Carly didn't like promises—giving or trusting them when offered—but, in that moment, she believed Noah's.

There was just something so simple and comforting about it.

So straightforward and reassuring.

It had been a long, long time since she'd gotten that feeling from someone, and it made no sense that it had come from a man she barely knew.

Yet it had.

Carly watched as his eyes dropped to his hand. He didn't take it away.

Suddenly its weight was all Carly could think about.

Its heat was all she could feel.

The world and its terrible troubles quieted.

How complicated would it be to kiss him?

To see if his lips provided the same escape that a simple hand on her arm had already made her imagine?

He *had* saved her life, right?

A kiss could show gratitude.

A kiss could show appreciation.

A kiss could—

Carly's phone rang one more time.

Noah retracted his hand.

For a moment she was tempted not to answer, but every wandering thought she'd just entertained was a reason to pick up the call.

She was on a case.

Her team was on a timeline.

There were bad people appearing in Potter's Creek with no hesitation to do bad things.

She had to stop them.

And that could only happen if she stayed focused.

Carly answered the phone. There was a touch of excitement in Opaline's voice.

"I hope you like karaoke, because this new lead I just got you is about to get musical."

Chapter Eleven

"If you had asked me what I'd be doing this holiday season, I don't think I would have guessed this."

Carly was a sight to behold.

Her lips were turned down, dark red and pouty, and her eyes were surrounded by black eyeliner and, if Noah wasn't mistaken, glitter. She had on tight dark jeans, instead of her slacks, that made the urge to let his eyes wander instead of be respectful a constant battle, and she was absolutely rocking a long-sleeved red blouse that dipped into a low *V* and made the imagination stand at attention.

It was a definite contrast to the natural beauty that was a part of her FBI look, but tonight Carly Welsh wasn't an agent.

She was just a woman on a date.

With him.

At a bar in the city, half an hour from Potter's Creek.

"Going undercover at a dive bar with a former Amish farmer to try to get information on a criminal who just escaped from the hospital?" Noah smirked. "I don't know about you, but this is how I always bring in the holiday season."

Carly had been stiff since she'd received the call about Rodney Lee's escape. That stress had stayed throughout her meeting with her team and their new plan to try to get a lead on Lee. Now she rolled her shoulders back and snorted, letting that tension go.

Or at least hiding it before they went inside.

"I knew you were mysterious, Noah Miller, but I didn't know you were *that* mysterious."

She took a deep breath and nodded. Noah started to lead the way, but Carly caught his arm. The smell of her perfume surrounded him. It was also in the distracting column.

"And, just for the record, I'm *not* singing on any stage, no matter what Opaline suggested. Ever," she added. "Not even for a cover."

Noah chuckled.

"Understood."

The bar was called the Wallflower and, despite its more hipster name, it had the look and feel of a motel bar located near the airport. This bar, however, was down the street from The Grand Casino and, given how the waitress greeted them after they sat down in a booth in the corner, it catered to patrons when they were done with their gambling.

"We don't take poker chips as payment. Only card and cash. If you can't do that then you can leave. No swiping our Christmas decorations, either, or you'll have to answer to the boss."

Carly shared a look with Noah. He could tell she was

fighting a laugh. The only decorations he could see that were holiday-themed were a few plastic light-up Santa Clauses on the bar top, clusters of candy canes with rope lights in them seemingly spread at random, and balding, metallic green garland lining the space between each booth seat and the next. It was more than he'd expected to see in the bar, but he wouldn't have thought it valuable enough to be targeted for petty theft.

Yet there the waitress was, serious as serious could be.

"None of that will be a problem," Noah assured her.

"We'll be on our best behavior," Carly added.

Another couple came through the main door, earning her suspicious gaze. Still, she took their drink orders. When she was gone Carly finally let out a little laugh.

She lowered her voice and leaned in so he could hear her whisper. The tabletop between them was small which put the smell of her perfume right back in Noah's area. He made sure to keep his eyes, once again, away from her curves at the movement.

Maybe volunteering to act as her undercover date while the rest of her team kept following their own leads down wasn't the best idea.

Yet, there they were.

"Is it bad I felt the need to go for my gun during that?" she asked. "I mean, dang, but I guess I can see how she might act like that if she has to deal with people like Lee as a regular."

At her own words, Carly looked toward the front doors. The waitress had directed them to sit in a booth that had a sightline of the entrance and the hallway opening that led to the bathroom and, he assumed, the back office and doors. The Wallflower wasn't particularly a large place, but it had several tables for seating between them and both exits. Noah watched as Carly scanned each patron sitting down with their drinks already.

"Not that I expected it, but Rodney isn't here," she said through a smile meant for a couple on a date and not an FBI agent trying to solve a case. "Neither is Rob Cantos."

Noah in turn did his own look around of the other patrons. The picture he'd been shown of Rodney Lee's friend, Rob, wasn't matching any of them.

"I still can't believe your tech guru found a connection," he admitted. "But I guess that's the pitfall of social media. One way or the other you wind up on the internet because of it."

Carly snorted.

"Especially if you're running around with someone like Rob, who obsessively posts pictures and videos on his Stories." The picture Carly had shown Noah was a selfie of Rob with Rodney in the background. It was, according to Carly's friend back at their headquarters in Traverse City, one of nearly fifteen pictures spread over the course of six months where the two had shown up together. Most of them were geo-tagged at the Wallflower. That had been enough of a lead for the tech guru to sleuth out that Rob didn't just like the small dive bar, he was a regular.

A regular who was there every night.

And if they couldn't find Rodney, then maybe his friend could help them with that.

"So you think he'll show?" Noah asked, making sure the couple two booths over didn't hear. "Rob, I mean."

"If his routine holds, yes." She checked the watch on her wrist. It was placed right where the bandage from the cut on her arm met the cuff of her sleeve. Noah had no doubt it was a strategic move to keep the bandage inconspicuous. She'd already used makeup to hide any trace of bruising or the small cut on her face. He'd had to do a double take to see if he'd imagined the wounds from the day before when he'd first picked her up from the bed-and-breakfast.

Though that second look might have been because of the simple fact that she was stunning.

However, Noah, who was more of a homebody than a bar hopper, hadn't had to do anything past leaving his cowboy hat at home and changing to a solid dark button-up instead of his normal flannel. Though he doubted anyone would recognize him regardless. He'd lived all of his life in Potter's Creek and this was his first time at the Wallflower.

"So, the plan is to sit here until he comes in," he summarized.

Carly nodded. "The team hasn't come up with a connection between him and the Amish community, so this is all we've got so far," she said. "Opaline said most of the pictures and videos he uploads from here are around eight to nine." She looked at her watch. "Which gives us a half hour to scope out the place, see if we can catch Lee or something suspicious and then see if we get lucky with Rob."

"And if none of the above happens?" Noah didn't want to be down about the plan but he genuinely wanted to know what happened next if it didn't pan out.

"Then we talk to the waitress and the owner. I'd do it now but since we're at a standstill with all other leads, I think this might be a better approach. We can't afford for anyone to rabbit because we spooked them."

The waitress appeared with their drinks. Noah waited until she was gone again to give Carly a humored look.

"To rabbit?"

She wrapped her hand around her beer bottle and smirked.

"It means to run. I dated a guy during the academy who always used to say it." She made a show of rolling her eyes. "We didn't last long, but that one phrase must have left an impression. I've had the entire TCD team poke fun at me for saying it over the last few years."

Noah had no reason to feel jealousy flare up at the mention of her dating, and he definitely shouldn't be curious if she was seeing anyone now, but there it was. Front and center before he could ignore it fully.

And before he could find a smoother way of figuring out how to answer if she was now single or not.

"So does that mean it's harder for you to date people in the same profession or do you have someone back home with a badge, too?"

Carly's eyes dragged over to his with a small, sliding smile.

He'd been caught.

"And here I thought Noah Miller was a dip-your-toe-in-the-water-to-test-it kind of guy and not a-jump-right-in guy."

Noah pulled his beer up to his lips and tried to downplay his guilt.

"I was just making conversation," he lied. "You *did* ask me yesterday if I was married, so I thought I'd learn a little about that side of your life, too."

"I said I didn't know that you were married," she corrected. "I never asked if you were."

Noah realized she was right. He nodded into his swig of beer. Carly took pity on him.

"But to *answer* your question, yes and no, and then no." She ticked off her answers with her fingers as she said them. "Yes it *can* be easier to date someone who's in law enforcement and deals with some of the same things I do, but *no* it can also *not* be easier. I once dated a guy who always tried to, for whatever reason, one-up me about work. He actually bet me he could go to the shooting range and outshoot me one time."

"And did you take him up on that bet?"

She smirked.

"We broke up out on the range after I won."

Noah laughed.

"Well done." She did a little bow.

"As for the last no, *no* I don't have anyone back home. Badge *or* civilian." Her humor fizzled a little. "This job can be…demanding. That doesn't always play well with the whole champagne flutes and long walks along the beach at sunset thing. But no harm or foul. Not all of us are made for that kind of life."

Her mood shifted, but not in the way he expected.

It was subtle. She looked down at her drink, her fingers toying with the edge of the beer's label. Then she went back to watching the patrons. Like what she said wasn't a big deal.

Just another somewhat useless stretch of conversation people put between the real issues.

Noah didn't want her to downplay what she'd just said by letting the subject change without acknowledging it.

He shrugged.

"Doesn't mean those of us who do cheap beers and dive bars with Santa decorations aren't the right kind of living, either. Simple isn't always bad."

Carly met his gaze with another subtle change. This one he couldn't read, but she tipped her bottle to him.

"I guess you're right there. I never was a woman fond of strolling any beaches. Too much sand, too many tourists. Speaking of extracurricular activities—" she motioned to the bar around them "—what does a normal night out look like for you? I've got a good idea of your day-to-day work life but I haven't really pegged how Noah Miller takes his messy yet styled hair down."

Noah chuckled at that, pleasantly surprised at how often Carly seemed to be able to make him laugh. He ran his hand through his hair for show.

"I'll take the hair compliment, thank you." Carly did another little fake bow, fluttering her fingers as if before royalty. "But as for letting it down, what I do for fun is just as simple as dive bars and beers. I like spending my time outside—hiking, fishing, the occasional building something with my hands. Sometimes I come out to the city for a drink or two with my staff, or go to their place to watch a game but, mostly, it's just me beneath the sun and moon."

Noah hadn't meant his answer to sound so *solitary* yet he heard the subtext in it before Carly's expression turned thoughtful.

"That sounds nice, but a bit lonely."

The past, *his* past, surfaced as quickly as a rising wave in a choppy ocean. It took too much of his focus to keep his body from doing what his heart wanted him to do—stiffen up and then retreat into himself. Right to the blue shed on the edge of the property that used to belong to the Tucketts. Back to the memory of the yellow house that was no longer there. Back to when he'd fought to leave a place he was told he belonged only to fall into the unknown.

An unknown that he had spent years making familiar.

Making home.

His home and no one else's.

Carly outstretched her hand and caught his on the tabletop next to his drink.

The feeling of fight or flight, to swim or drown, cleared in an instant. All Noah could feel was a hand smaller than his, warm and firm. Following it up to a woman who looked more serious than smiles.

"One person's lonely is another person's choice and no one can understand that choice until they've lived

"4 for 4" MINI-SURVEY

We are prepared to **REWARD** you with 4 FREE Books and Free Gifts for completing our MINI SURVEY!

Suspenseful Romance

Suspense

You'll get up to...

4 FREE BOOKS & FREE GIFTS

FREE
Value Over
$20!

just for participating in our Mini Survey!

Get Up To 4 Free Books!

Dear Reader,

IT'S A FACT: if you answer 4 quick questions, we'll send you 4 FREE REWARDS from each series you try!

Try **Harlequin® Romantic Suspense** books featuring heart-racing page-turners with unexpected plot twists and irresistible chemistry that will keep you guessing to the very end.

Try **Harlequin Intrigue® Larger-Print** books featuring action-packed stories that will keep you on the edge of your seat. Solve the crime and deliver justice at all costs.

Or **TRY BOTH!**

I'm not kidding you. As a leading publisher of women's fiction, we value your opinions... and your time. That's why we are prepared to reward you handsomely for completing our mini-survey. In fact, we have 4 Free Rewards for you, including 2 free books and 2 free gifts from each series you try!

Thank you for participating in our survey,

Pam Powers

www.ReaderService.com

To get your 4 FREE REWARDS:
Complete the survey below and return the insert today to receive up to 4 FREE BOOKS and FREE GIFTS guaranteed!

"4 for 4" MINI-SURVEY

1 Is reading one of your favorite hobbies?

☐ YES ☐ NO

2 Do you prefer to read instead of watch TV?

☐ YES ☐ NO

3 Do you read newspapers and magazines?

☐ YES ☐ NO

4 Do you enjoy trying new book series with FREE BOOKS?

☐ YES ☐ NO

Please send me my Free Rewards, consisting of **2 Free Books from each series I select** and **Free Mystery Gifts**. I understand that I am under no obligation to buy anything, as explained on the back of this card.

❏ **Harlequin® Romantic Suspense** (240/340 HDL GQ5A)
❏ **Harlequin Intrigue® Larger-Print** (199/399 HDL GQ5A)
❏ **Try Both** (240/340 & 199/399 HDL GQ5M)

FIRST NAME   LAST NAME

ADDRESS

APT.#   CITY

STATE/PROV.   ZIP/POSTAL CODE

EMAIL ❏ Please check this box if you would like to receive newsletters and promotional emails from Harlequin Enterprises ULC and its affiliates. You can unsubscribe anytime.

HI/HRS-520-MS20

the reason behind it." She ran her thumb along the top of his hand, soothing him while making her point. "So I'm sorry if that came out judgmental. It was more of an observation. I'm sorry."

She released his hand as quickly as she'd taken it.

"It's fine," Noah assured her after a beat. He shook the darkness off his mood and managed a grin. "It's no secret to me that I come off as a solitary creature most of the time. I think it took the Tucketts two years to convince me to go on trips with them for the farm. Even then I don't think I really talked much until I was older."

He hadn't said it for sympathy and the way Carly smiled, she wasn't dishing it out.

"Ah, the quiet kid routine was one I had down pat. It used to drive my parents crazy the first year or so I came to live with them. My dad ended up coaxing me out of my bedroom with promises of candy and old, crummy cop movies, and yet it still took a while before I said more than a few words at a time to them."

Noah's brow furrowed, wondering if he'd heard correctly, but Carly seemed to realize the confusion.

"I was adopted when I was eleven." Carly paused. Her eyes went to the label on her beer. She started to finally peel it when she returned her gaze to him. "They're really good people, and were amazing then, but my biological mother was killed when I was ten and adjusting was hard for a while."

A part of Noah that he couldn't really define softened.

"Oh, I'm sorry," he offered.

Carly did a little shrug. The label on her bottle was already half-peeled.

"A lot of people I've met in my line of work don't get there without some kind of traumatic event that changes everything. At least, that's how it went for me. One day I wanted to be an astronomer, charting stars all night, every night, and the next?" She motioned around them. "I'm Dr. Poison. A horrible nickname my last boyfriend gave me, but I guess that left an impression, too."

That's when it happened.

Like a rain cloud passing across a sunny day.

One second Noah was appreciating her, listening to her, and worrying about what *he* said and how *he* reacted to her. And Carly? She was doing what, he had no doubt, she thought was expected of her.

She had dipped into his past on accident and so she'd given a little of hers up in payment for it.

But then she'd slipped.

For whatever reason, she'd given more to Noah than she'd meant to give.

And it hadn't been okay, whatever the memory she had been sucked into.

Noah didn't know who Carly Welsh was a week ago but *tonight*, in this moment, he believed he knew her.

At least, in a way that felt more real to him than with any other woman he'd met.

So, Noah did something he hadn't planned on—though he would have been lying if he'd said the thought hadn't crossed his mind.

Just as she had done with him, he took Carly's hand in his, and locked his eyes with hers.

There was surprise and sadness and an X factor he couldn't understand yet, pulling him in to the woman who made dive bar and beers sound like the most appealing thing in the entire world.

He knew it was his imagination, but the world around them seemed to dim. When he spoke, Noah was already hoping she'd accept what he was going to do when he was done talking.

"I have no doubt that you, Carly Welsh, leave quite the impression yourself."

Then, in sight of a poorly lit Santa Claus figurine, he took Carly's chin in his hand and kissed her.

Like the bar around them, as far as he was concerned, the rest of the world fell away.

Chapter Twelve

Carly kissed him back.

The moment Noah's lips were against hers, it was like instinct took over.

Instinct mixed with a surprising amount of desire. Well, maybe not surprising, but definitely not what she meant to overtake her.

Yet, it did.

And right after a conversation she hadn't meant to have.

It hadn't taken her academy-taught profiling skills to realize that Noah had led a solitary, possibly lonely life. What's more, she'd acted on that by questioning him for a realization she was sure she had gotten right.

Then two things had happened at once.

Noah had started to shut down again, just like he had in the truck after she'd asked him why he left the Amish community. His expression of humor had wiped away and an instant tension had lined his body.

Carly hadn't liked being the cause of it.

So much so that, while he shut down, she did perhaps

the most startling thing since coming to town, or, actu-ally if she was being honest with herself, in a long time.

He'd been shutting down, so she started opening up.

Taking his hand, letting him know she truly didn't mean to pry and then feeling the weight of her own self-imposed walls had led her to a snippet of a story.

A nickname. An awful, accidental reminder.

Dr. Poison.

For all of her intentions to help ease Noah out of whatever she'd pushed him into, Carly had instead fallen into the trap of her own past.

Then it was Noah who had saved the day.

He'd brought her back to the present and out of her darkening, heartbreaking thoughts, with a caring, human touch.

Carly might not have known the man long, but *that* had been absolutely what she'd needed.

Him.

She'd needed him.

So Carly had kissed him back and, what's more, leaned deeper into it.

It was perfect.

That is, until the sound of a new group of patrons coming into the bar filtered into their bubble.

Perfect became ice-cold water to the face.

Carly's eyes flew open just as Noah broke the kiss.

He didn't say anything and she didn't want him to; instead they synced back up to the plan.

He took her hand again, adopted a cover-perfect smile and gave her the room to slyly examine the new group without both of them gawking.

A surge of adrenaline went through her in an instant.

"Bingo," she whispered. "Rob Cantos is in the house."

Rob was nothing like his friend Rodney. At least not in looks. While Rodney was a force to reckon with and filled with violence, Rob was stocky, short and a guy who looked like he laughed all of the time. His friends that followed him to a set of stools at the bar, however, weren't throwing out any vibes that Carly could work with. They were also more of Rodney's build. Just looking at their size made Carly's bruise beneath her foundation pulse a little.

"It looks like they're going to hang out at the bar," Carly said after a moment of watching the group. She used her free hand, the one not within Noah's hold, and took a long pull on her drink.

Noah's lips twitched at the corner.

"What? Never seen a lady take a drink of beer before deploying a ruse to question a person of interest?"

Noah chuckled this time. He made a show of doing the same with his drink.

Then it was all charm.

"And what if I said I had?" he asked.

"Then your dating life definitely was a lot more eventful than my 'to rabbit' guy."

He laughed again, but that humor was replaced with focus as Carly felt her own demeanor changing into work mode. They didn't even bring up the kiss.

Carly grabbed her purse as Noah placed a tip on the table. He let her take the lead as she scooted out of the booth and stood.

"Let's see if we can't just sweet talk our Mr. Cantos into telling us all about his friend."

RIHANNA DIDN'T NOTICE the camera in her room, but she did notice that her laptop had been moved right before she went to bed.

Before that, when she'd come back from the hospital after she'd spoken to hospital staff, deputies and then the sheriff of the county himself, she'd used her work laptop to go through some of the files Alana had sent her. Most were social media accounts to look into for a possible connection between Rodney Lee and David Lapp.

She'd gone through incident reports and community news looking for anything that stood out as suspicious or different enough to garner a closer examination.

By the time Carly and Noah had gotten their undercover idea approved—though including Noah had gotten considerable pushback at first—Rihanna had saved only three pieces of information that had struck her as odd compared to the rest.

The first was an incident report from the year before. An unidentified male, mid-twenties, light-skinned and dark-haired, had been seen spray painting a marijuana leaf on the side of an abandoned barn on land formally owned by the Kellogg family. He hadn't been caught and no more graffiti had shown up in the town.

The second was a social media post on the county's Facebook page. It was a call to arms for any tips or information on a teenager or young woman, no one seemed to be able to pinpoint her age, who had been seen as suspicious, hanging around Potter's Creek and then running before anyone could ask why.

As far as Rihanna could tell through the comments and following news story and investigation, the woman hadn't been identified, either.

The third tidbit of information that she found was the piece she really started to get excited about. It was a Facebook comment thread on a story about local business growth and tourism in which someone talked about a local real estate developer who wanted to open up a dude ranch in the middle of Amish country. Half of the people who commented had been vehemently against it—there were enough farms in town to begin with and The Grand Casino in the city was as close as they wanted to be to more tourism—while the other commenters had been supportive but realistic.

One woman had said that, while she might have liked the idea of getting more outsiders into town to shop at her local boutique, there was no way that the Amish families would sell out to an Englisher.

Rihanna might be a liaison, but she'd been an agent first. Her knack for keeping the peace in her current job hadn't softened the edges of knowing a good lead when she heard it. Or, in this case, read it.

She'd emailed the screenshot of the conversation to her phone and hurried downstairs to the kitchen. The owner of the bed-and-breakfast, Dot, a lover of gossip but professional as far as Rihanna could tell, was getting ready to go to her house behind the inn for the night and looked elated that she'd been interrupted. Not.

Rihanna was apologetic but then got down to business.

While Carly was doing the right thing by being sly to get clues, Rihanna had long since run out of coffee and was in no mood to be coy.

Which seemed to be fine by Dot, considering how quickly she reacted to Rihanna mentioning the realtor who had tried to start a dude ranch not too far from the inn.

"Yeah, that was Caroline Ferry," Dot said with a huff. She slung her dishrag over her shoulder and took a stance that exuded grumpiness. "She's this rich lady who lives in an honest to goodness mansion. I mean that place is three times the size of this inn and she's not even married. I heard she has a staff of five. Boggles the brain to have that much space with only one person."

Rihanna mentally locked away the name Caroline Ferry and pushed past Dot's obvious annoyance.

"So why didn't she start the ranch? If she has a lot of money, couldn't she have bought what she needed to make that happen?"

Dot shook her head, but there was a smirk on her lips.

"She wanted to build along the creek which ran smack dab across three different properties, owned by three different Amish families. Three farms. Those families turned her and her money down flat. From what I've heard through gossip at the market, she tried to appeal to each of them, but in the end she had to scuttle the project." That smile grew. "I guess she found out the hard way that sometimes principles don't have a price tag on them."

"Do you happen to know which farms those were? What families, I mean?"

Dot didn't have to think twice. She listed off the names like she was a contestant on *The Wheel of Fortune* and she was going for a solve she knew.

"The Kline family, the Weaver farm and the Graber farm." Dot hung her head a little, sympathy spreading across her expression as Rihanna had alarm bells start ringing through her head. "I guess now if she wanted to try again she might have a better shot, since Elmer and his son passed."

Rihanna nodded.

"I guess so."

She said good-night to Dot and sent Carly a text to call her when she was done with her short undercover stint. Then Rihanna went to her room to call Opaline.

That's when she noticed something was off.

When she'd left her laptop it had been tilted *just enough* to where she could look out of the window with a glance instead of turning her head while working. Now it was centered.

Such a small thing, yet Rihanna paused.

Had she done it?

She turned to look back at her bedroom door. She hadn't locked it when she went downstairs, since no one other than FBI agents were staying inside.

Surely no one had come inside the room without asking.

Or maybe you've had too little sleep because you've too many questions bouncing around in your head.

Rihanna turned back to the laptop and decided to go with what she was sure about.

She called Opaline.

"Multitasker extraordinaire, Agent Lopez here," she answered. Rihanna laughed.

"Glad you're feeling feisty about it," she responded. "Because I need you to look up the address of a Caroline Ferry and anything odd that might stand out about her. When you have that, call Carly and tell her what you've learned."

Opaline might have had fun, but she was always professional when it was called for.

"Sure thing. Want me to send it to you, too?"

"Yes, please." She looked back at her laptop. "And send it to my phone only—text me."

Opaline didn't question it.

"Will do."

The call ended and Rihanna stood still for a moment in the middle of the room before sitting down in front of her laptop again. She slid it a little to the side again for an easier view of the window.

This time she made sure she noted exactly where it was.

He watched through the feed as the boy almost destroyed their plan. As soon as the woman left the room, the boy had taken advantage and hurried to the laptop. He'd already tried the other rooms during the day, but the agents either had their laptops in their vehicles or they hadn't used them at all.

This Ms. Clark was the only one who had been seen through the feed plugging away at hers.

But before the boy could do more than open it and

see that a lock was set up, he must have heard the liaison coming back up the stairs.

Panic had registered on his face seconds before he'd done something that not even the man would have attempted.

The boy had crawled beneath the bed to hide.

He was there now, beneath the floral-patterned bed skirt, less than a foot away from a woman whose sole purpose while in town was to take down the people behind the attacks on the community.

Which was why he couldn't let the boy get caught.

He sighed into the dark and picked up his gun, but not before looking back at the monitors.

All agents were snug in their rooms.

All except Agent Welsh.

Like the boy, she was another problem he was going to have to deal with.

And soon.

Chapter Thirteen

The rain came in the middle of the night and turned half of Potter's Creek to ice. Trees were encased by it, and windshields were annoyingly coated, but that didn't stop the community from getting up and out. The main roads were salted and still drivable once the windshields were thawed, and a horse-and-buggy were seen in the distance before Carly and Axel went in the opposite direction.

They had a job to do, though the new bite of cold wasn't helping Carly's mood.

It, like their case, was in flux.

From anthrax to David Lapp's basement to Rodney Lee escaping the hospital, every few hours a new problem popped up without a solution.

Then there was the whole kiss thing.

Noah had instigated it, yet Carly? She'd reciprocated.

And she'd wanted more.

That was as troubling as it was confusing.

Why did she feel a connection with someone she barely knew? That's not how the world worked.

Yet, she'd woken up thinking about the farmer. Just as she'd fallen asleep thinking about him, too.

It hadn't helped that the night before had driven home Carly's growing suspicion—she and Noah were a good team. He'd played his part as her date when they'd gone to talk to Rob Cantos and his friends at the bar. Rob had been an outgoing guy and had looped the two of them in for a round of drinks and a lot of idle chatter.

Noah had been the one to steer that talk to the questions they had needed answered. All without arousing any suspicion.

They'd found out that one of his buddies had fallen so hard for a girl that he'd left everything behind to come to the city to be with her. Something Rob hadn't been a fan of, from the way he said it.

"Having a lady is one thing but his focus was over one hundred percent," he'd said. "When he wasn't drinking with us, he was all about her. And even when he was with us?" Rob had tapped his temple with his finger. "He was still with her."

That's when Carly had finally shown her badge. She got more pointed with her questions and Rob hadn't had too much of an issue parting with the answers. It turned out he'd been talking about Rodney and Rodney wasn't one of his favorite people, just one of his group and that group had an order to it. One where Lee was bottom rung.

Rob had had a name for the girlfriend and a place she worked, but hadn't known where Rodney had been staying.

"Do you know exactly where all of your drinking buddies live?" he'd asked when Carly had pushed.

"I can at least point you to a zip code."

At that, Rob had shrugged.

"When we hung out it was here." He'd pointed to the front doors and then to the bar. "He'd walk in through those and sit down here and then just leave when we were done. The most I got out of him was posing for a few pics." He'd then dragged his eyes to the notepad in Carly's hand. "Plus, the quickest way to find Rodney is to find Talia. No matter what he's done, he won't leave her alone for too long."

So that was the information she'd decided to act on as she waited for news from the labs analyzing the anthrax samples she and the team had sent them. Preliminary analysis hadn't turned up anything especially unique or pointed to a trail they could follow.

Find Talia to find Rodney.

Which was starting to feel like its own investigation, an issue Carly hadn't bet on when they'd left Traverse City.

Potter's Creek sure hadn't let up on its surprises and curveballs. Not even while the TCD team had been in their rooms, ready to turn in.

Which was a big reason why Axel was frowning now behind the wheel,

"I've worked cases where I've effectively been in a war zone and felt more at ease there than here in this small town." He rolled his shoulders back. "Bioterrorism, shady development deals, bad boyfriends, Amish flying the coop. What's next, plagues of locusts?"

Axel's boyish charm was absent. He needed more sleep, she guessed, judging by the bags beneath his eyes. That and the fact that, while she'd been at the Wallflower Bar schmoozing up Rob, the team had been startled awake by several gunshots outside of the bed-and-breakfast. Three to be exact.

It had been enough to send every TCD agent to their service weapons and out into the night.

By the time Noah had dropped Carly off, they had just been finishing their search.

"It could be a hunter?" Carly had offered. Selena, in her matching pajama set, had shaken her head.

"Not for this time of year and not for here."

"It could be someone trying to rile up a building full of FBI agents," Max had guessed. "It's not like there's all that much to do around here. I imagine the youth have to get creative to get their rebel jollies off." At that, Aria had raised her eyebrow. Max had laughed. "What I mean is that it could have been out of boredom, too. A few shots into the dark to feel alive."

Axel, however, hadn't been so sure.

"Check it out in the morning," Carly had told Selena. "Just to make sure it wasn't something else."

Then they'd gone back into the inn and made a new game plan for the next day thanks to the information about Talia and the gossip Rihanna had gotten from Innkeeper Dot.

Now Carly was with Axel and almost to Caroline Ferry's mini-mansion, a residence that was somewhat secluded from the city, but the drive didn't take them that far away from the inn. It still had a good amount of trees surrounding it and, judging by the ride up the private drive, it was one of a kind in the area.

Almost like an estate fit for a celebrity.

"She's a realtor, you say?" Axel asked. He leaned toward the steering wheel to make an exaggerated show of scoping out the place. "Is she also a hired hitman for the mafia? A drug kingpin? A movie star rehearsing a role?"

Carly snorted. She looked down at her notepad and the notes she'd taken from her call with Opaline.

"According to our dear Lopez sister from afar, Caroline Ferry was a self-made real estate developer…before she exponentially increased her worth by marrying a man twice her age who had a trust fund that would put some small countries to shame."

Axel whistled.

"I was about to say, if she got all of this land and square footage from real estate, then I'm definitely in the wrong business." There was an actual half circle drive that led right in front of a set of double doors, like it was a drop-off in front of a hotel lobby. Two other cars were pulled off to the side beneath a portico. Both were sporty, but neither looked particularly new. Though Carly would have been wholly surprised if they were anything less than a hundred grand each. "Does one of these belong to Mr. Ferry?" Axel had his eyes on the two-door, slick red car closest to them. There was clear appreciation in his voice.

"No. Two years after they married he passed away from natural causes associated with old age."

Axel turned the car off and shook his head, looking longingly one more time at something he'd probably never buy for himself.

"Who knew all we had to do to get a place like this and cars like that was to marry rich and old."

"A lot of people know that one, Axel," Carly mockingly chided. "Gold diggers are real." She dropped the mocking in her tone. "Though it is extremely rude, insensitive and judgmental of us to think that's the case for Ms. Ferry before we've even met her."

Axel's grin came back.

"Don't worry. I won't judge anyone until they give me a reason."

They exited the car and were met at the front door by an older woman wearing a gray uniform with an apron. She was quick to introduce herself as a member of the cleaning staff and showed them inside and back through to a study where she lingered, as if awaiting orders.

All of it was grand and, try as Carly might not to, she formed an opinion about the woman who owned it all before setting eyes on her.

Caroline Ferry was absolutely in the top 1 percent when it came to wealth.

And she was proud of that fact.

Just as much as she was unbothered by two FBI agents being led into her home office.

"I've had a lot of people in my house before, but I don't think I've had any members of a task force. What did you say it was called again?" she asked after looking at Axel's and Carly's badges.

Axel put his badge back into his pocket. Carly followed suit as she scanned the room around them. It, like the house, was done to the nines. Modern, smooth, bright surfaces, trinkets that screamed attempts at artsy sophistication and several paintings with frames so ornate Carly bet they cost more than her apartment's rent. There were built-ins that ran the length of one wall, while the exterior wall was mostly window. It showed a view of a beautifully landscaped backyard with what looked like a lap pool in the distance.

Even Ms. Ferry matched her home's opulence. Her platinum blond hair was twisted back in a flawless bun against her head while her lipstick, manicure and white dress with gold accessories were stunning in their execution.

Ms. Ferry was certainly the most well put together suspect Carly had ever interviewed before, that was for sure.

"The Tactical Crime Division, ma'am," Axel answered, all polite. While Carly was the lead agent on this case, she followed his cue on how to speak to the woman. He was the expert profiler after all. If he went polite it wasn't because he was after an *Emily Post* etiquette award.

He did it because it was easier to catch flies with honey. Not vinegar.

"Do you mind if we take a few minutes of your time for some questions?"

Ms. Ferry swept her arm back to two love seats, also equal parts elegant and immaculate.

"Oh absolutely, why don't we take a seat. Hetty?" The woman in the apron straightened, as if at attention. "Could you get us some refreshments, please? Would you two like some coffee?"

Carly was quick to decline because she had been caught off guard by the specific offer. Too quick. Axel gave her a look while he accepted.

Then it was the three of them in the study.

"I bet I know why you're here," Ms. Ferry started. "It's because of that nasty business with the poisoning."

Carly nodded. She wasn't surprised that the woman had brought it up. There was no other reason the team would be in town.

And with such simplicity.

Ms. Ferry touched her chest. She shook her head and breathed out. The very picture of exasperation.

"I can't believe something like this would happen in our own backyard. I mean, Potter's Creek is a stone's throw away and those people are so *modest*. I can't believe someone would do that to them and for what? It's not like they have anything. Unless maybe it was a hate crime? You know, Hetty and I talked about that. Surely no one around here has a problem with the Amish that badly. Then again, what a crazy world we live in. I mean I heard about two men fighting in the casino not too long ago because of Amish values. *Values* for goodness sake! At a casino no less! Honestly, what *is* the world coming to?"

This time Carly couldn't hide her reaction that Ms. Ferry was being open and friendly. In fact, not a whiff of suspicion had come off of her yet. She wasn't nervous. She was meeting their gaze and keeping it. In fact, if anything, she seemed excited for them to be there.

Carly shared another quick look with Axel.

He cleared his throat, bringing the woman's attention back to him.

"When you say they don't have anything, that's not exactly true. They have land. Some land you were actually interested in not too long ago."

Ms. Ferry nodded so quickly that Carly was sure her hair was going to come undone.

"Yes! The Graber farm!" She got to the edge of the love seat and spoke like she was starring in a soap opera. "When I heard what happened, I couldn't believe it. First the family is hurt, and then that beautiful land? So tragic. I wanted to reach out to them but it didn't seem right, and it's not like I could just pick up the phone to call."

"You wanted to reach out to them? Why, if you don't mind my asking?" Carly followed up.

Had Ms. Ferry tried to swoop in to buy the land from the remaining Graber family? That certainly would give credence to her having motive.

Yet, Carly was having a hard time believing Ms. Ferry was their culprit.

The older woman waved her off, like asking was no problem at all.

"I wanted to express my condolences." She sobered a little. "One widow to another."

The answer seemed genuine, but they had a case to

solve and too much time had already passed without any answers.

So Axel followed up with a little more pointed series of questions.

"And what about seeing if she would sell you their land now, after everything had happened?"

That seemed to perplex her.

"What do you mean?"

Axel went at it again.

"They are one of three families who refused to sell their land to you so you could build your dude ranch, right? With their cattle being killed, their land being affected and their main workers gone, you have way more leverage to convince the Graber family to change their minds."

Ms. Ferry's brow furrowed. Just as she seemed genuine in her desire to commiserate with the Graber matriarch over being a widow, she seemed to be genuine in the confusion that followed.

"The dude ranch project was tabled. The Grabers were one of three families who refused to sell. So I let it go when it was clear they weren't interested at all." For effect, she shrugged. "I've turned my attention back to some other projects outside of Potter's Creek since then. I even have a flight booked after the start of the new year to go to Tennessee and talk to a friend about turning my focus to more charitable pursuits instead."

"So you're not interested at all in the dude ranch anymore?" Carly asked. "Just like that?"

Ms. Ferry nodded. Then her demeanor changed. She

lowered her voice. Not to a whisper, but not as flamboyant as she had been.

"Honestly, I came up with the project on a whim in the first place—I mean the scenery around here is like being in a movie, why would I not try to capitalize on that if I could?—but it was my son who really ran with it."

That was news.

"Your son?" Axel asked.

"Yes. Dylan." Once again, her demeanor changed. She definitely was no longer feeling whatever excitement she had been before. "He's had a…rough time of it lately, and so I told him that if he cleaned up his act and flew straight then I'd let him be in charge of the entire ranch when it was up and running. Something he could call his own and that would give him a sense of purpose."

Carly and Axel both straightened a fraction. Carly saw it out of her periphery just as she knew he had seen her.

"What do you mean by cleaned up?" she asked.

"And what do you mean by rough time?"

Shame.

Guilt.

Frustration.

All three flashed across Ms. Ferry's expression and perfectly applied makeup.

"Dylan's father, my first husband, had a drug problem when Dylan was younger. After we divorced, Dylan went through a sort of rebellious phase…one that included gambling." She deflated a little with a sigh. "He's been in and out of different rehab programs to kick his addiction to it over the last few years. It got so bad that I had to…cut him off. No more money from me. He was going to have to learn how to fend for himself. I thought that it would help him value the things he earned himself, instead of seeing them as just more ways to fuel his addiction."

"Did he follow through?" Axel asked. "Did he fend for himself?"

Ms. Ferry sprung back up like a flower in spring. She was out of her mood.

"He did! He completed a program, got himself an apartment, kept going to meetings and told me he was ready to take on more responsibility."

"But then you ran into the issue of getting the land to build," Carly added.

Ms. Ferry frowned.

"He took the news poorly, I'll admit." She sighed. "Which is why he's in a rehab facility in Austin, Texas, at the moment. He relapsed after I broke the news to him."

After that they asked a few more questions, but none with answers that led them anywhere new. They got alibis from Ms. Ferry for the time frame when the attacks were estimated to have occurred and learned enough about her personality to make the leap that she hadn't been behind the attacks.

She also didn't know David Lapp or Rodney Lee.

"What is it about this case?" Axel asked when they were back outside. "If it is just one case we're looking at right now."

"You think it could be two." It wasn't a question. In fact, it was a theory the team had already kicked around. "Our original anthrax attack case which leads us to David Lapp who is somehow mixed up in something different with Lee. Which makes David Lapp our soft connection?"

Axel gave a half shrug.

"I know we're not big on coincidences, but that doesn't mean they don't happen."

Carly didn't believe Lee wasn't somehow connected to it all, and same with the still-missing David, but she didn't have any proof one way or the other.

Like Axel said, just coincidence.

And he was right. She wasn't a fan of those. Not in their line of work. Yet, if it was…if something else was going on unrelated to the anthrax killings…

Another attack could come soon and hurt more people.

"Until something else happens, I'll keep Max and Aria on trying to find out how the anthrax was transported and purchased, and I'll check in again on my lab sources to see if they've found anything more about the strains used," she decided. "Once Opaline finds Talia, you and Rihanna head over there with local PD as backup. If Rodney is there, take him in. If it's just Talia, question her for every ounce of information she has on Rodney, David, and if she knows anything about that damn chair in his basement."

Axel nodded. His approval of the plan gave Carly an added confidence boost. She was staying objective in his eyes.

Which was good, because her last part of the plan didn't feel as professionally detached as it should have.

"Before then, I need to pick up my rental and head to the Miller farm. I need to ask for our tour guide's help one more time."

Chapter Fourteen

Gina had her shotgun on the kitchen counter. Noah had a cup of coffee. Both were staring at Carly with their full attention.

"You two have lived around here your whole lives, right?" she asked. It was a one-question follow-up to her asking if she could come inside to talk.

Noah had been hoping she'd stop by—for what he wasn't sure—but it was an easy yes from him. Gina also seemed eager to talk, something that was definitely rare from the closed-off woman.

"Yes, ma'am. In this county and the next," she answered.

Noah nodded along.

"On an Amish farm and then on this one. Why?"

Carly had something rolled up beneath her arm. She motioned to the dining room table across from them.

"May I?"

"Go ahead."

They all circled the table while Carly unrolled a good-sized map. It was laminated and looked like a Potter's Creek–wide survey. The top corner read that it had been drawn up in 2012 but, from a quick first pass, it appeared to be more or less the same as the town now.

Carly pulled out a dry-erase marker, held up her finger as a 'hold on' sign and started to draw a line on the plastic. Noah and Gina leaned over and watched as that line started at the town limits, then went directly into backstreets through town for a bit, before moving to a network of back Amish-land roads that led to the Yoder, Graber and Haas properties. Then she was done.

"That's the route I would take if I was bringing in enough anthrax to poison three families." Carly tossed him the marker. Noah caught it with one hand and an eyebrow raised. "Now, as locals, you tell me how you would do it."

Noah shared a look with Gina. Her gaze was already on the map.

"Well, first of all, if I was coming from anywhere outside of town, I wouldn't take these." Gina pointed to the first network of backstreets. "I'd take the main road as far as I could before turning off of it."

"And why is that?" Carly leaned over again. Her hair shifted at the movement. Noah noticed that she'd gone back to her more natural look while working. While he wasn't against her undercover style, he liked the sight. Her focus and determination to get to the bottom of the case was more appealing to him than glitter.

"The main road has less traffic than the back ones do around that area, believe it or not," he explained, agreeing with Gina. "Plus there are a few one-lane neighborhoods those open up into. If you drove an unfamiliar car around there, especially at night, it would stick out more." He drew a line along the main road and paused when he got to another that split through the heart of the Amish community. Instead of following Carly's line through the backroads she'd chosen, he drew his own while Gina made sounds of approval next to him. When he was done at the Yoder farm, she took the marker and got back to the road that went through the heart of the Amish community and went to the other side of the map, leading away from the town's main road.

Carly pointed to the first change Noah had made.

"Okay, explain why you went there."

"It's not really about why I went there, it's why I didn't go *there*." He tapped her original plan. At least, one road in particular. It didn't have a name on it. "That's the road that runs behind the Kellogg property. It's abandoned now, which makes it a good, out-of-the-way spot, but—"

"That's the road you said gets so muddy it's pulled wheels off of buggies," Carly finished, remembering their earlier conversation from their tour.

Noah nodded.

"Even when it's not muddy it's pure hell on a regular vehicle. No local would use it unless it was on foot or they had no other choice. Not with an unnecessarily high possibility of breaking down or damaging your vehicle."

"And what about leaving after the deed is done?" she asked Gina. "Why would you leave Potter's Creek on this side of town and not the other?"

"Even if you came in that way, I'd leave that way,

too. Cops are never on that road. Don't ask me why. It's just been that way since I was a girl."

Carly didn't say anything for a moment. Noah watched as her gaze swept the map, thoughtful. Her wheels were spinning.

"Does that mean you think it really is David Lapp behind it? Someone who grew up around here?" he finally asked.

"I honestly don't know at this point. Everyone is out there chasing down leads from what we learned last night and from what we already knew coming into the case." She tapped the map. "But spreading that much anthrax on that much land requires a lot of work, labor and at least one vehicle large enough to transport it to and from." It also required someone who knew how to spread it without risking self-contamination, something she'd already mentioned to the team. The health and safety group tasked with mitigation had suggested this to her as they'd worked in Hazmat suits, cleaning up the fields. "If you're right then, if a local did it, they would take a completely different path and, if someone who wasn't local did it, then—" she ran her finger across the plastic until she was on the road behind the Kellogg property "—maybe they made a mistake we haven't looked for yet."

The thoughtful silence that followed ended in a flash. She rolled up the map and gave them both a quick smile.

"Thanks for this," she said, already backing up to the door. He realized with a start that she was about to leave.

Without him.

And he didn't like the feeling.

For a lot of reasons.

"Do you need me to come along?" he offered, coming around the table and trying to avoid the intrusive gaze of Gina caught in the middle.

Carly hesitated.

He might have imagined it, but it sure did look like Carly had turned a darker shade of crimson.

Gina spoke instead.

"You should take him," she said. "You'll make a good team. A local and an out-of-towner, like you said. You'll probably see more with him tagging along. Plus, he already helped me mend the fence this morning and that's all I needed from him today."

Gina cracked a grin at that. Noah snorted.

"She's right. About both of those things."

Carly seemed to think about it for a little longer than Noah liked, but then she agreed.

"You can make sure I don't destroy my rental on these backroads."

"I think I can swing that."

Noah drank the last of his coffee and offered Carly a cup. She hesitated, then declined.

It was the second time she'd stopped and started with indecision just within the last minute.

Probably because you kissed her out of nowhere during a damn FBI investigation, he chided himself. *The one guy from the community tasked with helping her and you lip-locked her at a bar.*

Noah didn't regret the kiss, but he did regret how it had happened. The fact that they hadn't talked about it at all since then, not even in the car ride back to the inn, didn't help. It also didn't help that he'd spent the morning waiting for her to show up or call only to have to remind himself several times over that Carly Welsh wasn't in town for the scenery.

She certainly wasn't there to fall for the shunned farmer of Potter's Creek.

That had been a wise, rational reminder.

Though thinking about Carly falling for him? Well, that was a slippery slope right into another question: If he was wondering about her falling for him, did that mean that he was falling for her?

Was that possible?

To have such strong feelings for someone whose middle name you didn't even know?

To know something in your heart before your head got the memo?

Now Carly was standing next to her rental, peering down at her phone, brow furrowed and lips downturned.

It wasn't a special moment, in fact it was downright normal.

Yet, it happened all the same.

One moment he was looking at her and, in the next, he was thinking about the yellow house and dreams for his life.

It was the second time in his life that he'd felt exactly what he was feeling now.

And *that* to him was the most surprising thing that had happened so far in Potter's Creek.

"So Opaline found Talia's address and Axel is there now with the city PD." Carly didn't look up as she spoke. Noah didn't think he would have been able to hide the feeling unraveling in his chest if she had. "I'm hoping that means we can finally figure out this whole Rodney Lee and David Lapp thing at least. Give us some solid ground to work with."

Noah cleared his throat and went to the passenger's side of the SUV. A new excitement was emanating from Carly as they got in, and she turned the engine over and started out of the drive.

"If we can get Talia to talk, then I'm hoping we can be done with Rodney and David."

"You don't think David was responsible for the attacks now?" he asked. They hadn't talked about the case at all after he'd dropped her off at the inn the night before. The map discussion with him and Gina was the only talk about it they'd had since their night at the bar.

"At this point, I'm hoping what we do or don't find during this little trip will help point us to a local being behind this or not." She slapped her hand against the steering wheel. "Wait! I didn't even tell you about what we found out today, did I?"

Noah laughed.

"No, ma'am, you didn't."

"Well hold onto your butt and listen to this."

Carly told him all about Caroline Ferry and her son, Dylan. Noah had met Caroline once at the market but hadn't known much past the fact that she hadn't been able to convince the families to sell. He'd never met her son or her late husband.

"So what would Dylan's motive be?" Noah asked when she was done. "Trying to get back at the community as a whole for messing up the deal? Or maybe scaring those who hadn't sold to try to sell now?"

"Neither option makes that much sense. Again, getting and spreading that much anthrax, and not even against all of the families who stopped the development before it could even begin, is a lot of work. Especially for an uncertain outcome. Then again, I've seen people who are startlingly good at the follow-through and nothing else." She sighed. "But, while Dylan would be my lead suspect now, he couldn't have done it. He's been at one of those fancy rehabs in Florida for two months. At least that's what his mother said. Opaline is chasing that down, too, just to cover all of our bases."

Carly ran a hand through her hair. He thought she was going to sigh again, yet she caught herself with a light laugh.

"You know, with all of this going on, I keep forgetting Christmas is days away," she continued. "I actually think I would have forgotten completely had Dot, the innkeeper, not reminded me before I left this morning by filling up the kitchen with platters of Christmas tree–shaped cookies." Her laugh this time dipped a little. "I always think one year I'll nail the whole holiday spirit and have this big party with all my loved ones and Secret Santa and all the Hollywood stuff you see in sitcoms. Like I'd really put the effort in and feel it. Yet, here I am having to be reminded by cookies that this year it's not happening."

"Well, this Christmas you're also working an attack that was first flagged as bioterrorism, right? That would take the holiday cheer right from anyone's sails, I'd think."

Carly moved her head back and forth, like she agreed and didn't all at the same time.

"One thing I've been learning, and I think the rest of my team has been trying to learn, is the whole light and darkness balance of what we do."

"See the good in everything so the bad doesn't crush you," he guessed.

She nodded.

"So, sure, I'm in Potter's Creek investigating a biological attack with a lot of unknown variables and seemingly unlimited questions because of those variables, *but*—" Noah caught her gaze as it swept to him. Just as quickly, she looked back out the windshield. "It sure is pretty here."

Noah couldn't help but laugh.

"That's one thing Potter's Creek will always have going for it, thick or thin   it's hard not to see its beauty through it all."

"You've got that right. I mean, I love my apartment and my job, but if I woke up to this, even just on the weekends?" She motioned to the forest in the distance, blue sky framing the expansive field in front of the trees like a painting. "I think finding the good in life might be easier."

Carly had no idea how much she'd just affected Noah with her words. They reached through his attraction to her, his respect and awe at her dedication and wit, and landed next to a younger version of him, trying to explain to an entire town why he didn't leave Potter's Creek.

It made him smile.

Really smile.

Because Carly had no idea she'd just given him something he'd been wanting almost his entire life.

Understanding.

"Maybe I can cook you dinner tonight." Noah heard himself say it before he realized how out of the blue it sounded. He hurried to expand. "I mean to try to bring some stress-free dining to a stressful case. And, well, to thank you for everything you've been doing because you might not ever get that from anyone else here."

Carly tensed. Noah was worried he'd overstepped *again*. He went back to looking out of the windshield to give her privacy to come up with a way to say no.

"Maybe if I play my cards right Dot will let me bring over some Christmas cookies."

There was a smile in her voice.

Noah chuckled.

"I wouldn't say no to that."

Their personal conversation switched gears as Noah directed them to the road that ran behind the Kellogg property. Carly pulled over onto the grass.

There was no more talk about Christmas cookies or finding the light in the darkness.

She got out of the vehicle and went right up to the dirt road, eyes down and focused.

Noah went farther down from her, eyes also on the road.

He didn't have to be a trained agent to see what she was seeing.

"It looks like someone wrecked out recently," he said when Carly showed up at his side.

"You said this road gets awful when it snows or rains, right? It's done both since I've been here, but if someone carrying a heavy load spun out in the mud? Then it might still be here for us now."

Noah agreed. It looked like someone had gone too fast and lost control enough to use up the entire road before going into the grass, kicking up chunks of both along the way.

"So if this was the person who was carrying the anthrax—" he started.

"Then I'd bet my badge that they weren't local," Carly finished.

Chapter Fifteen

Answers.

What Carly had been looking for since before their plane touched down.

She wasn't even picky in the beginning about how many she could get.

Just *one* would be nice.

Instead the questions came. The ones that were standard: Who was behind the attack? How did they do it? Why?

But then they split into more, complicated questions: Where was David Lapp? How was Rodney Lee involved? Were they connected to the anthrax attacks?

Never mind Carly falling prey to her own personal questions: Why was Noah Miller so attractive? Why couldn't she stop thinking about him? Had his offer to make her dinner been meant as a date?

As many questions as she had piling up, Carly nearly jumped for joy when a few answers found their way to her while inside David Lapp's bedroom an hour later.

Axel walked around the room, looking for something, clearly excited as he spoke.

"Talia's apartment was empty," he said after she walked inside. "But not *empty*. It was like someone had ransacked the place, looking for something. Just like in here." Ransacked was an understatement. Max seeing David's bedroom through the window had been the reason why they'd first come inside the house in the first place. The room looked like a tornado had torn through it. The team had done a search after their first encounter with Rodney at the property, but now Axel and Carly were taking a second look.

"So, wait." Nothing was making sense to Carly. "Who do you think was looking for something?"

Axel kept moving things around, latex gloves a flash of blue as they crossed over the mass of clutter.

"At first I thought that maybe David somehow connected with Rodney and his girlfriend and took something from them. Then they came back here to try to find it. Or vice versa. Talia has no priors but since Rodney has a drug history, I was thinking maybe David might have gotten tied up in something like that with him."

"At first," Carly repeated. "What do you think now?"

Axel's spine zipped up, standing straight as an arrow. There was something in his hand. It was a picture, but he didn't show her right away.

He was grinning.

That *I got something* grin.

"This room and Talia's apartment were both basically trashed in the same way. There was anger and aggression. Things were destroyed even though there was no real reason to do it."

"Whoever was looking for something was pissed, is what you mean."

Axel handed over the picture.

"I think it was Rodney, but I don't think he was looking for *something*. I think he was looking for *someone*."

It had been folded several times, making creases across the face of a young woman. She was sitting on the floor, back leaning against a small bed. Just by looking at the picture, Carly was left with the impression that the woman was shy. Reserved. Holding back but still smiling.

She reminded Carly of herself.

"Who is this?"

Axel's grin of knowledge only spread.

"That's Talia Clark." He stepped aside and motioned to the bed, flipped over on the floor, the wooden posts broken with unnecessary force.

"And that's the same bed from the picture," she realized.

Axel nodded.

"You said Rob Cantos used the word 'obsessed' when describing how Lee talked about Talia. He even seemed put off about the relationship, maybe subconsciously so."

"Yeah. None of them seemed to be fans."

"I think that's because it wasn't a two-sided kind of love. On a hunch, I had Opaline look into Talia's medical history and in the last two years alone she was admitted three times into the emergency room with a concussion, a broken rib and a fractured cheekbone."

"Rodney was abusing her."

Carly could still feel the occasional throb of the cut on her arm that the man had given her. Her body was still sore in places from him using his sheer power against her.

Believing he was an abuser wasn't at all a stretch of the imagination.

"But all three times she was quoted saying it was because she was clumsy and nothing more."

"So she didn't report him."

He nodded.

"She doesn't have a support system, which couldn't have helped. Her father passed away when she was in middle school and she aged out of foster care." His excitement dulled. Carly understood the feeling. Having a lead was great, but a lot of the times the lead itself was heartbreaking.

Axel pointed at the picture then thumbed back at the bed.

"Now what if, at some point, some way, David Lapp meets Talia?" he continued. "What if they become friends or fell in love?"

"His father said he was kicked out of the community for lying, stealing and sneaking out," Carly realized with a start.

"Going against the tenants of your religion and jeopardizing your entire life and connection to your family? That's not something you usually do unless there's a really good reason."

Carly looked down at the smiling Talia.

"Unless it's for love."

Her thoughts split two ways at once.

She imagined David Lapp giving up everything to be with a girl.

Then, almost in sync, she thought about Noah.

Is that why he had left the community?

For a girl?

For young love?

"I could be wrong but I think David Lapp was helping Talia hide from Rodney, and I think Rodney knew it," Axel said. "That's why this place is trashed. He was looking for something, but was pissed about it. He probably did the same at her apartment trying to figure out where she went."

Carly shook her head a little. Not because she didn't think his assessment was right—in fact, she believed it was the truth as soon as he said it—but because there was still one piece of the David Lapp puzzle that didn't make a lick of sense.

"But what about the chair in the basement?" she asked. "That took time and forethought. Two things I'm not so sure Rodney Lee would have had if he came looking for David and Talia. I'd think, based on this mess, that he's more of a punch first, ask questions never kind of guy."

At that, Axel sighed. He looked around the room then shrugged.

"If David was here, and the dried blood is any indication, Rodney could have tortured him for information on Talia. But you're right. The setting up for the chair doesn't match up with the profile I've made of Rodney."

"Unless he had a partner." Carly didn't want to say it because it only made everything more complicated.

Yet, since the first moment she'd seen the chair, she'd felt something about it didn't fit.

"If that's true then where are they and where are David Lapp and Talia now?"

Another round of questions.

Carly added to it.

"And are they connected to the anthrax attacks or did we accidentally step into another case altogether?"

"I don't know, but it sure feels like somewhere in the world a clock started ticking a lot faster."

Which was Axel-speak for they were running out of time.

For finding David Lapp and Talia? Carly wasn't sure yet.

But at least they had a profile and good guess on the David Lapp situation and Carly was going to count that as an answer.

They shared a small silence, both processing their own questions, when a bark sounded outside. Selena and Blanca were on the lawn. Selena had another answer to another question when they came outside to meet her on the porch.

"I found bullet casings in the woods outside of the inn," she jumped in. "From a .22. CSI came in to grab them but while I waited, Blanca and I took a look around the area." Selena's nostrils flared. "There are a lot of footsteps leading to the tree line that has an unobstructed view to the front of the inn."

"And when you say a lot…" Carly started.

"I mean at the very least three distinctive prints, despite the rain and snow we've gotten since being here," she finished.

Axel's brow pulled in together.

"Which means whoever was out there, they were out there recently," he said. "Someone's been watching us."

"It could be out of curiosity, and the shots could just be boredom or rebellion like Max guessed," Carly said, playing the devil's advocate.

Selena shook her head. Something was eating at her. Something she didn't care for.

"There was another trail that branched off from the original cluster that were fresh. I followed them right up to the back porch of the inn."

That got the hair on the back of Carly's neck to rise a little.

"You think one of our peeping Toms came in for a closer look?"

Selena's lips thinned.

"Who's to say they just stopped at the porch?"

Carly didn't like that thought. Not one bit.

THE THIRD AND fourth answers Carly was given felt more solid. She had relocated to the community barn and had been jumping between calls when Max's number showed up on the caller ID.

"We found the van, the one the perp used."

Carly actually squealed.

"You did? How? And where?"

"Since you told us about that road being harsh on a vehicle, we threw a Hail Mary and called around to see if any of the mechanics had a work order on a van or truck."

"That would be incredibly stupid not to just destroy the vehicle and move on," Carly had to point out.

"Exactly, *unless* you borrowed or rented the vehicle because you needed something bigger than you had."

"So they loaded their vehicle with anthrax and then took it to a mechanic to fix because it got busted up a little during delivery?" Carly could hear skepticism coming out clearly in her own words.

"Oh, there were no vans or trucks brought in to be fixed," Max corrected. "But there *was* a work order that the boss flagged because it was a little on the unusual side."

"Oh?"

Max waited a beat for dramatic effect.

It worked, because Carly scooted to the edge of the chair she'd been on.

"Someone called in asking for the name of the best car detailer they knew and offered big bucks to have them come do it on site *and* as quickly as possible."

Carly could feel an adrenaline surge coming. One that came with leads actually leading to something tangible. Something they could use.

"And do we know who made that call?"

Max's voice fell a little.

"Not yet, but we did trace where the call came from and where the detailing job took place. In fact, I'm standing in front of the *van* right now. Can you guess where we are?"

Max didn't give her the time. Which was fine by

her. She was all about getting answers sooner rather than later.

"We're in an underground parking garage beneath The Grand Casino. And, Carly? It belongs *to* the casino. As far as we've been able to see, it has been checked out for maintenance for over a month."

"Can they prove where it was during maintenance?"

"We're running that down now but, based on how quickly they're calling up the food chain to the big boss, I'm going to take a stab in the dark and say they actually had no clue where it was until they found it down here all clean and shiny like brand new."

Carly chewed on her lip in thought. If anyone had been in the barn with her, she bet she would have looked more than a little disoriented as she ran all the questions and theories through her head before she finally landed on what she wanted to happen next.

"We need to find out who took the van in the first place, who had access to it, any security cameras that clocked it coming in and out of the parking garage, and a list of employees if it wasn't stolen." She stood, adrenaline now in full surge. "I'm coming your way now. I'll let you know when I'm there."

They ended the call and Carly went around collecting her jacket, keys and credentials, so focused on the new information that she almost didn't see the woman until she was right in front of her.

"Sorry," she said. "I knocked but I don't think you heard me."

Carly scanned the woman in a flash. Her dress was long and beige and a bonnet was wrapped on top of light brown hair in a tight bun. Her face was devoid of makeup but filled with worry. It showed on her as she wrung her hands in front of her. Carly thought the woman looked to be in her late-forties.

"It's okay," Carly assured her. "How can I help you?"

The woman looked like she wanted to say a lot but, instead, seemed to choose her words carefully. Her eyes skirted from Carly's gaze to the ground as she spoke.

"I know you are looking for who was behind the attacks and I think I found something today that you should see."

"What is it?" That definitely wasn't what Carly had been expecting. Not only was someone from the community talking to her, the outsider, but she was trying to help.

"I wasn't supposed to tell you so we need to hurry," the woman urged.

A look of fear swept across her expression.

It propelled Carly forward in an act of comfort through close proximity.

The woman looked like a scared animal about to bolt. And Carly wasn't about to scare her off.

"What did you find?" she asked, making sure to keep her voice low and soothing.

"I'm—I'm not sure, but let me take you there and you can see for yourself." She paused. "Only you. I only trust you. Please."

Carly looked at the woman, *really* looked at her.

She'd seen something, all right.

That much was clear just by her body language.

Never mind the worry and fear written across her face.

Carly had to go.

Maybe she would get her fifth answer for the day.

"All right, show me."

Chapter Sixteen

Noah started cooking early.

Gina eyed the progress from the kitchen bar with an eyebrow raised but her opinions off. That was, until she caught Noah checking his phone.

Again.

"She's got a case to work," she finally said. "The sun hasn't even set yet. Stop counting the minutes or the hours are going to feel worse."

"I'm not counting the minutes," Noah defended.

Gina didn't buy it.

"You're not the laid-back, relaxed Noah I'm used to seeing, either. Is this dinner you invited Agent Welsh to a friendly one or romantic?" She made a point to look at the countertop. He'd pulled out all the good dishes, which meant real plates were out on the dining table. Something he planned to set up when he was waiting for stew to finish later.

Not exactly normal behavior for him.

"Friendly," he said, all gruff.

Gina snorted.

"You may say that word but I think you're hoping for

the other one." Gina, who had never been one to nag him about the romance department, took a surprising stand. "I like her."

His surprise must have shown. She rolled her eyes.

"I can like people, thank you very much," she added. "It just doesn't happen often."

"I think the word *you* mean is 'ever.'"

He smiled as he said it because there was no version of him that would ever talk down to or about the Tucketts. They'd given him a safe place to learn who he was and what he wanted out of life, only ever asking for hard work and respect in return. Both of which he'd been glad to give as he made a place in the world for himself.

Gina tossed a pen from the counter at him. It was a playful move that he laughed at as he dodged the projectile. It hit the floor and skidded into a box sitting on the floor of the open pantry. Gina leaned over to get a better view of it.

"Is that our old Christmas box?"

Noah had never been one to blush, but he did feel some heat move up his neck. He'd forgotten to hide it before Gina had come in for a break.

"Yeah. I was moving some things around in the attic and found it."

He went to the box, gently pushed it into the pantry, and shut the door. Out of sight, out of mind.

But not for Gina Tuckett.

She was the hare after the carrot.

"But why is it in the kitchen and not the attic?"

Noah could have lied, maybe should have, but there

was no use hiding from the truth. Not with the woman who was basically his older sister.

"Carly was down about missing out again this year on the holiday spirit, and it doesn't help she landed a case in the middle of an almost-entire town that doesn't celebrate. So I thought I'd look to see if I couldn't put up some more decorations. It's the least I can do."

Gina's eyes narrowed. Not necessarily in a bad way, just an analytical one. She opened her mouth to, no doubt, dive into the reason behind his actions when a knock sounded against the front door.

All curiosity went from questioning the good to worrying about the bad. They shared a look, then Gina was off of her stool and scooping up her shotgun. Noah grabbed the iron skillet he'd been about to prepare, then led the way to the front. After all that had happened so far, neither of them were taking any chances.

On either side of the oak door were two narrow floor-to-ceiling windows. Through one of them, Noah saw who their unexpected guest was.

"I can count on one hand how many times he's been to this house in the last decade or so." Gina's voice had gone sour. Noah had a more complicated reaction within him.

Noah made her lower her weapon and handed over the skillet.

Then he opened the door, not at all knowing what to expect.

"Dad?"

Samuel Miller wasn't a large man, but he was solid. An entire life of working with his hands, a life spent

avoiding help or shortcuts combined with a loyalty and
dedication to his beliefs, made him a presence stronger than any Noah had ever encountered. Then again,
maybe Noah's perspective was skewed considering he'd
grown up around the man.

And then disappointed him by leaving the faith and
life he'd cherished above all.

Now his father stroked his beard and looked as uncomfortable as Noah was confused. He gave Gina an
equally uncomfortable nod of hello.

Then he was back to his son.

"I need to talk to you. It could be important."

He glanced back at Gina.

"I'll go make sure the kitchen doesn't burn down,"
she said, catching the hint. "Yell if you need me."

When she was gone, Noah motioned inside.

"Do you want to come in? We can go to the office."

His father shook his head and instead took a step
back.

"Out here is fine."

Noah wanted to ask if being so close to where his
son lived, and Noah himself, offended his father that
much but decided now wasn't the time. Even if it had
been, it wouldn't have mattered.

Like Gina said, his father had only ever been to the
Tuckett farm a handful of times since Noah had moved
in. Nothing had changed when Noah had taken the farm
over, either.

"What's going on?" he asked, moving so they were
in front of two rocking chairs that Mr. and Mrs. Tuckett
used to sit in on Sunday nights after dinner.

His father stroked his beard again.

He didn't like what he was about to say. That much was clear.

"Your brother, Thomas, came to me earlier today and said he hadn't seen Aaron in two days."

Noah's brow furrowed. The name sounded familiar, but with everything going on it was harder to place than normal. His father helped him out.

"Aaron is Abram's youngest son."

Noah cocked his head to the side a bit.

"Abram *Lapp*'s son? As in David Lapp's brother?"

His father nodded.

"Your mother heard about the investigation into David and your talk with Abram, so I wanted to make sure everything was okay with them myself," he continued. "So I went to talk to Abram. He was still out working, but I found his wife, Willa." He let out a long breath and looked like he'd rather be any place but right there, telling an outsider his problems. "I've known her as long as I've known your mother and I can tell you something was wrong."

"As in she didn't know where Aaron was, either?"

"As in she told me to leave and not come back after I expressed concern."

"Did she ever say where Aaron was?"

His father shook his head.

"No. Given everything that's been happening, I thought to come to you with this." He started to say something but must have changed his mind. "Aaron is a good boy, Noah. We need to make sure he's okay."

"Agreed. Come inside so I can call Carly."

His father didn't fight the offer, but Gina met them in the hallway before they could make it to the kitchen. She already had his phone.

"An unknown number is calling."

Noah took the phone. He didn't have time to wonder whom it could be before a man's voice came through with such acute concern, Noah's gut hardened into worry.

"Is this Noah Miller?" the man asked by way of hello.

"Yes, and this is?"

"It's Axel. Agent Morrow." Noah was about to ask what he could do for the man, but Axel barreled into the reason for the call. Then the worry made sense. "Is Carly with you?"

"No. She's not."

There was no hesitation.

"Do you know where she is? When's the last time you talked to her?"

Noah didn't like these questions.

Gina and his father both watched his expression with concern.

"The last time I saw her was when I dropped her off at David Lapp's house to talk to you."

"So you don't know where she is."

"No. You don't?"

Axel let out a string of expletives that would have tested the faith. Noah was close to it himself when the agent answered.

"No, we don't. She was at the barn the last we talked. Then she was supposed to meet us here at The Grand Casino an hour ago. Now no one can get a hold of her."

"Let me guess, she doesn't normally do this on a case."

"No. She never does this."

Noah went back to the kitchen and grabbed his keys. Gina and his father followed. Both of their eyes widened when he grabbed the shotgun.

"Then it's time we find her."

CARLY HAD MADE a mistake in letting the beautiful scenery lull her into a false sense of security. She wasn't in a postcard. She wasn't vacationing with her adopted parents or spending the weekend buying beautiful handmade furniture at an Amish market.

No. She was investigating a biological attack on a community.

And it had been naive to think them all innocent.

That had been another mistake she'd managed to make. She'd forsaken years of caution, skepticism and the perspective to see the big picture beyond the details.

Now the years of personal and professional experience were flooding back in, like a river reclaiming the land past the dam it had just broken through.

Carly had made a mistake.

And she was about to find out how much it was going to cost her.

The breeze picked up and pushed a sheet of her hair along her cheek as she followed the Amish woman through a field to a barn after Carly had driven her to this spot. She didn't move it out of the way. Her focus had become a net, one she threw around the barn and now was pulling back to her. She was listening for a snag. Something out of place. A clue. A reason why her gut had gone from calm to alert in a second flat.

And why the woman who had led her there hadn't yet given her name.

Carly unholstered her gun, but kept it low at her side.

The moment she pulled it out was the moment she realized it wasn't loaded.

How was it not loaded?

How had she not noticed?

You put the holster on with it still in there this morning. But did you actually hold the gun?

Carly didn't have an answer for either.

But she hazarded a guess as to who the stranger was walking ahead of her, leading them to the side door of the abandoned barn. It was a half mile from the stretch of road that Carly and Noah had inspected earlier that day.

The Kellogg property.

The abandoned barn they hadn't yet checked.

"I never caught your name," Carly stalled, attention still sweeping the area as best she could.

The woman kept walking. She hadn't been a fan of looking Carly in the face.

Not a sign of being shy or reserved.

It was something more.

How did you not see it before?

"Oh, I'm Katherine."

Her words were flighty.

Adrenaline.

Fear.

Guilt.

The closer they got to the door, the more she was losing the facade of innocence that had made Carly feel safe.

That had made Carly underestimate her.

"I don't think it is."

The woman hesitated. The door was a few feet from them. She walked to it, but stopped before her hand could go for the handle. Carly lowered her voice to a whisper only they could hear.

A few of the puzzle pieces to the larger picture were falling into place.

Too bad Carly was alone for it.

"I think you're David Lapp's mother, Willa." The woman turned to look at Carly so quickly she almost flinched.

She was definitely afraid.

"I don't know what you're talking about."

Carly made a show of holstering her gun. Not that it would do much harm without the bullets. Another problem for another time.

She held up her hands to show she was harmless and took a slow few steps forward.

"I think that you're David Lapp's mother, and whatever is inside of this barn is a trap. I'm guessing from the man who's looking for him or maybe the man who already has him." She took another small step forward. This was the woman Carly had seen through the window of the Lapp house when they'd tried asking questions about David Lapp. "Because I think the only leverage that would make a woman forsake her faith, lie and be a bystander to violence is a serious threat to that woman's family."

The woman glanced at the door, then back at Carly.

"You have to go into the barn," she stated. Like she was reading a script.

Carly was just as firm.

"I'm not going into that barn."

The woman, who now Carly was positive was Willa Lapp, shook her head.

"You *are* going into that barn."

"It doesn't have to be this way, Willa." Carly reached for her phone.

No one knew where she was. Not her team.

Not her boss.

And not Noah.

"I can help you," Carly stalled. "I can help David."

Willa shook her head. Fear, guilt, anger. Carly couldn't tell what she was looking at anymore, but when Willa spoke Carly knew what she was hearing.

A mother who loved her son.

"He was missing for two days before I found a cell phone with the video of him being taken on it. You showed up three days later." She shook her head. "You are late to this game, Agent Welsh, and I'm not willing to bet his life on you being better at it than *him*."

Carly should have run.

Or fought.

She should have done something the second Willa opened up.

But those damn answers were there again, taunting her.

So, Carly rolled the dice and tried to get some.

"Him? Him who? Rodney Lee?"

Willa was good. She looked like she was thinking about answering when really she was just stalling. When her eyes skirted over Carly's shoulder, it was already too late.

Carly had made mistakes.

And her life was now the cost.

Chapter Seventeen

Waking up in pain was a shock to the system.

Waking up in pain and seeing someone you didn't expect to see, staring at you, was another one.

Waking up in pain and finding yourself hanging from a complicated pulley system where your wrists were bound around a giant metal hook?

Well, that was a nightmare within a nightmare.

Carly's head was throbbing as the details lined up with the pain she was feeling. On reflex, she wrapped her fingers around the hook so that the weight was off of her wrists alone. That alleviated some of the pain.

But definitely not all of it.

Carly sucked in a breath as she looked down.

Three details filtered in late.

All of them were terrifying.

She was hanging a few feet off the ground, above what looked like snow but she knew instantly was none other than the poison that had brought her to Potter's Creek in the first place.

Anthrax.

It coated the barn floor beneath her in a messy circle.

That alone would have made her blood run cold.

But then there was the detail that her jacket was no longer on her.

Neither were her shirt, jeans, socks or shoes.

She was hanging there in her black set of underwear, cold air against her skin.

Another not-so-great development.

Yet, the third detail that combined with her pounding headache changed everything.

She'd been cut along the tops of her thighs and, what felt like, her back. Not too deep, not a lot of blood, but definitely three lines of open wounds.

Which meant that Carly was absolutely exposed to a biological agent that killed through exposure.

And the person who had set up the theatrical trap?

They knew the fastest way to kill someone with the poison.

For the briefest of moments, Carly thought about her mother, but then a man cleared his throat from a chair near the side door.

Carly wasn't surprised that Rodney Lee was leaning back with a gun resting against his leg and a smirk on his lips.

"I got worried you were hit too hard and weren't going to wake up." His eyes scanned her body up and down. If she wasn't bouncing between pain, fear and anger, she might have added disgust to the list. "Not even the knife got you going."

Carly took her own time to look around.

Willa was nowhere to be seen.

"Don't worry, your friends won't interrupt us," Rodney continued. "It'll take your team half an hour, at least, to get back from the city. That's if they even know where to look. That's the good and bad thing about not being local. We're all just bumping around in the dark after a while."

Carly didn't like how Rodney had gone from the behemoth in the woods, all aggression, to a man who sounded like he was enjoying hearing himself speak.

She was in pain.

And extreme danger.

She didn't have the patience to listen to the bad guy banter with himself.

So she got to the point.

Or *a* point.

"Why did you attack the Amish? Was it punishment for David Lapp helping Talia escape from you?"

Rodney was a hundred or so feet away from her, from the anthrax. Even at that distance, she saw the anger in him flare to life at the mention of David's name.

"Talia didn't *escape* from me. He tricked her. Took advantage of her. *I'm* the one who's trying to save *her*."

That was surprising, a feeling that was starting to lose its edge on account of how many surprises had been springing up since arriving in Potter's Creek.

Did that mean that he still hadn't found Talia?

What did that mean for David?

"So you haven't saved her yet?"

Rodney growled—actually *growled*—at her.

"That little punk hid her like it's some kind of game. And you think I'm the dangerous one."

Carly winced as the cold air made her shiver.

If any of the powder kicked up and made it to her…

Adrenaline surged through her again. It was going to exhaust her faster than her fear.

How was she going to get out of this?

You can't do it alone.

The one resounding internal thought chilled her even more because it was right. She needed help to get out of this without being infected.

She needed her team.

She just hoped they'd raised the red flag when she hadn't turned up at the casino. Though she didn't know how long she'd been in the barn unconscious. If Rodney had already set up the trap before she'd gotten there, then hoisting her up on the pulley and spreading the powder had to have taken some time, especially if he was to remain safe from the deadly substance.

Stalling until they found her was her best bet.

"Where did you get the anthrax?" she asked. "It's not the easiest thing to get, even on the black market. Or to know how to deal with safely."

Her arms were starting to burn at trying to stabilize her weight in suspension. Rodney was acting like they were having a normal conversation instead of him sitting near a circle of poison, talking to a woman hanging above it and dripping blood.

Axel would have loved to add that to his profile of the man.

"You'd be surprised at the secrets people share when there's enough money involved. And you can look up anything on the internet, you know. Even how to handle this stuff." He nodded toward the powder.

Carly didn't doubt that.

She also didn't understand the why of it all.

"So, let me get this straight—" Carly bit back a small yip of pain as she shifted to try to get more comfortable. A losing battle, she knew. "—you're trying to find and punish David for hiding Talia. But didn't you already have him? You kidnapped him and then had him in that chair in his basement, right?"

At that, Rodney stood. She couldn't read his expression as it went from anger and indignation to something akin to being thoughtful, a look that didn't really fit him.

"His family saw that he was up to no good with Talia and everyone shunned him for it. Having him taken to his own house was the only place we were guaranteed not to be disturbed." That anger came out again, quick and hot. "I almost had him talking when you and your friends showed up to town."

"You left," she realized. "And David escaped. Didn't he?"

There was that growl again.

He took a step forward, gun in his tightened grip and aimed at the ground.

"I underestimated him. I won't do that again."

So David was still out there.

But why hadn't he come forward?

Were he and Talia gone?

And, more importantly, why was Willa helping the man who'd taken and, she assumed, tortured her son?

Carly wanted to ask—wanted to get to the bottom of something—but it was clear that whatever Rodney had been building up to was close. He did another slow look up and down her body.

Then his gaze dropped to the floor.

He grinned.

"But *you're* not getting away from me."

This wasn't like when Carly was in the woods with the man. Where she felt no need to accept that she might not make it out alive. This was different. She was absolutely vulnerable.

Carly thought of her mother again.

An ache that never left became more pronounced as an old anguish ran through it. She didn't want to, but it made her think of her father.

What would he think when he found out his daughter was killed in a similar way to his wife?

Would he be upset?

Or would he think it poetic?

The daughter who helped send him to prison for poisoning her mother, poisoned herself.

It sent a wave of regret through Carly.

Then defiance.

She didn't want to give him the chance to feel anything when it came to her.

That defiance rolled into a building rage. It came out at the man who still didn't make sense to her.

"Why the theatrics? You could have disappeared. Why grab me in the first place? Why do *all of this* and chance being caught?"

Carly's voice rose at every question until she was all but yelling.

Rodney was unaffected. His smile stayed in place. His gun, however, didn't.

He moved it up, so it was aimed at her head.

"You were getting too close."

That wasn't an answer Carly wanted.

But the writing was on the wall.

Rodney Lee was done with talking. He was done with her.

Carly closed her eyes, refusing to let her last moment on Earth happen while staring at a vile, violent man.

If she had to go out, she'd rather go out in darkness behind closed eyes.

And, at least this way, poison wouldn't be the end of her.

Carly took a small, quick solace in that.

"Don't move."

A deep baritone cut through the cold air like the gunshot she'd been expecting.

Carly opened her eyes as a flurry of motion took place at the back of the barn.

Noah Miller had come through the side door with a shotgun trained on Rodney. He glanced over at Carly but didn't address her. His focus squared up on the man who had frozen, gun still aimed.

"Now lower it or I'll shoot," Noah commanded. The sheer power and authority in his voice surprised her.

It made something in Carly actually flutter.

But there was no time to feel anything more.

"You won't shoot me," Rodney said. "It's against your religion."

Everything happened all at once.

Rodney pulled the trigger, just as Noah pulled his. Carly yelled, expecting to be there one second and gone the next.

Yet, no new pain came and neither did a kill shot.

Rodney's body was blown back, then crumpled to the floor.

There was no way around it.

He was dead.

"Carly?" Noah's voice was filled with panic as he turned to face her.

She was ready to say she was okay—other than the obvious—but then a peculiar sound followed an odd sensation coming far above her.

Carly craned her head back to look.

"Oh my God, he shot the rope."

Rodney's bullet hadn't been meant for her head.

It had been meant to sever the rope above the hook and have her fall to the ground.

It was a lot of trouble to go through to make a statement.

But man, was it effective.

"Noah! I can't touch the ground!"

Panic spread as quickly as the rope was unraveling.

Noah sprang into action. He threw his gun down and started over.

"You can't touch it, either," Carly warned.

Noah came to a halt right outside of the circle of powder. He looked around the barn. There wasn't much to work with and there wasn't time to figure out a way to work with what there was.

Carly could see it in his expression.

There wasn't a way to grab her without risking exposing himself.

And Carly realized with such a strong force ramming into her chest the she didn't want him to risk it.

To risk himself.

She wanted Noah to be safe. To be healthy. To decorate his Christmas tree with so many ornaments and bobbles that the branches weighed down and sagged from the weight.

She hadn't known him for long but there she was, accepting exposure instead of wanting him to risk himself.

That meant something. A lot, in fact. It also didn't stop Noah from being himself.

He stripped off his coat just as Carly dropped down half an inch.

"Don't touch it," she warned him.

He didn't listen.

The rope gave way with a small snap. Carly didn't have time to yell.

Noah, however, was fast.

He ran through the powder and caught her before she could touch the ground. Sheer power kept both of them from being causalities of momentum. Instead he held her like a bride, his jacket beneath her.

Carly didn't have time to react.

Not yet.

"Walk very carefully out of this," she ordered instead.

Noah nodded and did as he was told.

He held her against his chest, bleeding and in her underwear, until they were outside. The cold hit harder now that the barn's walls weren't there to cut through it.

Carly realized she was shivering.

It took her a few seconds longer to realize it wasn't all thanks to the cold.

"Are you okay?"

Noah's voice rumbled through his body and into hers.

Carly opened her mouth to try to convince him that she was, especially now that he was there.

Yet, what came out next was something she hadn't let out in a long time.

Tears.

They poured out of Carly like the waters behind a broken dam. Her body shook which made all the pain worse.

"It's okay," Noah soothed. "I got you."

Somehow that relief only made her tears worse.

THE BOOTS WERE goners.

They were burned outside of the abandoned barn as a hazmat team, CSI, and the Tactical Criminal Division and local law enforcement surrounded the area. A fire truck showed up, but it was Selena Lopez who rushed Carly to the hospital.

Noah, too.

He slid into the back seat of her rental SUV without shoes and still holding Carly, wrapped up in his coat.

She insisted she was fine, but the dried blood against her skin and swollen and red eyes would have been enough to convince anyone otherwise.

Never mind that she had been *dangling* above enough anthrax to kill her.

"They're going to make sure you're good and you're going to let them," Selena had barked at her. It was obvious she cared for Carly and Carly felt the same. She gave in and didn't argue as they sped to the city.

"How did you find me?" Carly had asked instead.

"Axel called and said they couldn't find you. Your tech guru found out the last place your phone had been active was off of the road behind the Kellogg property. I realized we hadn't checked the barn yet. Then I saw your rental."

Carly nodded against him.

He could feel her wince.

He also felt her jump as she remembered something.

"Willa Lapp got me to the barn and when I realized it was a trap she admitted that David had been taken a few days before we came to town."

Noah stiffened. He felt her look up at him to see why.

"When Axel called me, my father showed up at the house. He said that my little brother was worried about his friend Aaron, David's brother. When Dad went to go talk to Willa about it she turned him away."

"Once he told us that we sent local PD out to their place," Selena added from the driver's seat. "Right before I got here, Axel got a call that they had Levi in custody but that Willa and Aaron are still missing."

Noah, who had only been in contact with Axel before he'd gone to the barn and right after he'd gotten Carly, had apparently missed a few steps the team had gone through in that time.

"Does anyone know where David is?" That was still a resounding no. Carly sighed. "Rodney didn't, either."

"Maybe he and Talia left together," Noah offered.

Carly's voice was quiet when she spoke again.

"Maybe."

The rest of the ride, Carly recapped what had been said in the barn while Selena updated her on what she'd missed at the casino.

"They said they wouldn't have known the van had been missing at all had we not shown up. There were no security cameras in the area it was originally taken from *or* returned. Opaline, Amanda and Alana were looking into any traffic cams or footage from surrounding businesses that might have caught the driver leaving with it or coming back when we realized you'd gone missing. The man who detailed the car said he was paid in cash left in a bag next to the car. Aria called the number he was originally contracted by and it was the landline at the Wallflower Bar."

That got Noah's attention.

"Where Rodney liked to drink on occasion," he said.

Selena nodded.

Carly wasn't as enthused.

Not that he blamed her given what she'd just been through.

"So it was all about Rodney's obsession with Talia? The anthrax attack on the community and abduction of David? And then stringing me up in an abandoned barn?" Noah felt her skepticism pouring off of her and onto his chest.

"You don't like this," he stated.

"It just seems like a lot of unnecessary trouble and work for an outcome that he still wasn't close to getting," she said. "It doesn't make sense."

Selena sighed.

"Just because he was bad didn't mean he had to be smart about it."

At that, they agreed.

Still, Carly was unconvinced.

She was quiet for the last few minutes of the ride.

Noah tried to ignore how warm she was against him.

Chapter Eighteen

Carly decided that, once and for all, listing things she hadn't expected to happen while she was in Potter's Creek was a useless pursuit.

Rodney, David, Talia, anthrax, the Grand Casino and the Kelloggs' abandoned barn? All unexpected.

Meeting Noah and *feeling* for him the way she was? Definitely unexpected.

Waking up in his house smelling like his body wash to the faint glow of a bedside lamp shaped like a horse shoe?

Carly decided there was no reason to deep dive with rhetorical questions about how she'd gotten there.

The short but eventful journey from touching down at the airport, to being beneath the sheets of a bed-and-breakfast's bed with a bandage around her arm, to being beneath the sheets at the Miller farm with a few more bandages and soreness had admittedly been a wild path.

But one she didn't regret for a second traveling, unexpected or not.

So she palmed the cell phone on the small side table

and sat up. It was almost two in the morning and there were no new calls or texts.

Carly hadn't meant to sleep this long, but she was glad she hadn't missed out on anything. Then again, their bad guy couldn't hurt anyone anymore. He was gone.

Wasn't he?

Carly's three new wounds stung a little as she moved. The doctor at the hospital had confirmed none of them had been deep. He'd disinfected them and bandaged them with a stern warning that if she felt off at all to come back immediately, then put her on strong antibiotics just in case. But, as far as they and their tests could tell, she hadn't been exposed.

Neither had her savior.

That had somehow meant more to her.

A sound of movement from the other side of the house pushed the haze of sleep out of her in an instant. She got up from the bed and took her phone out of the bedroom, alert.

That feeling of fight or flight ebbed as she approached the kitchen. By the time she was next to the dining table, it was all but gone.

"Oh my God," she breathed out. Noah froze in front of the middle of the kitchen, his hands full. Carly laughed. "What is all of this?"

Selena and Axel had both agreed at the hospital that they would feel better if Carly stayed with someone they could trust while she got some rest. They'd meant Noah and he had quickly agreed. Carly hadn't been able to deny she liked the idea, too, especially while she slept. She felt safe with Noah around.

When they'd gotten the okay to leave and come back to the farm, Gina had even still been up and in the kitchen, right where Noah said he'd left her. She'd made his dinner that he'd been planning to make Carly and the three of them had eaten in companionable silence. Carly had liked it.

The warmth of the kitchen, the quiet of the house.

But now?

Now the kitchen was an explosion of reds, greens, silvers and golds. Garland and tinsel and little paper trees and candy canes. Ornaments decorated the table centerpiece while a crimson-and-green table runner stretched beneath it. A Santa hat sat on the counter, beneath it one of four place mats covered with embroidered snowflakes.

The cherry on top of the extremely festive look?

Noah holding a baking sheet filled with Christmas tree–shaped cookies.

"I was hoping you'd be asleep a little while longer." He put the cookies down on the countertop next to the sink and looked like a child who'd just been caught trying to sneak a peek at Santa. He motioned to the holiday decorations around him.

"Originally I was thinking of putting some decorations out for our dinner but, well, after everything that happened Gina offered to run out to the Walmart in the city and grab something better than what we had here."

Carly was still in awe at how festive everything was.

She walked over to him, staring at the garland he'd strung along the tops of the upper cabinets.

"But why?"

Noah looked, dare she think it, bashful.

"I thought it might be nice to give you some holiday cheer." He checked the time on the microwave in the corner. He turned his head to do so. It was all she needed to get in front of him. "Since it's past midnight—"

This time it was Carly's turn to give a kiss that wasn't expected, the moment he turned back to her.

Every ache or pain in her body quieted, just as the bar had around them when Noah had touched his lips to hers.

And now it was Noah who kissed her back.

Warm. Soft. Brief.

As soon as it started, it was over.

Carly stepped back and met his hooded gaze.

She didn't want to leave him, but she did want to give him an out.

Just because she wanted him, didn't mean he still wanted her.

There was still a lot she didn't know about Noah Miller, and there was still a lot that he didn't know about her.

Yet, being in the barn and thinking about her mother had changed something within Carly. Or, maybe, shifted was the better word. She loved who she had become, despite her trauma. She loved her job, her team and the ability to fight for justice for those who couldn't always get it themselves.

What she hadn't acknowledged to herself, until she was staring at the man who had refused to leave her side in the hospital, was how she'd put up barriers to love.

It was easy to fake it, to go through the motions, and she'd done a good job of that through the years. Dated off and on, but never got too far. She'd had an excuse ready for every relationship's end. Usually she blamed her job. Sometimes she blamed the men. But most of the time? It always boiled down to one fact.

Carly didn't open up.

Not fully, not ever and not even to the people closest to her.

And she wanted that to change.

Starting with Noah.

"I don't let anyone make me coffee because when I was ten my mother died of arsenic poisoning," she started, jumping right into her personal hell. "The doctors didn't know why she was sick until after she died and realized she'd been poisoned slowly for weeks. The detective on the case figured out that it was something she ate or drank every day, and anyone who knew my mother knew how much she loved coffee. What *I* knew was that my father always made it for her." She took a small breath. "I don't let anyone make me coffee because my father used it to kill her. He took something she loved and used it as a weapon to punish her for his own unhappiness. Then I helped put my father in prison for life and was placed in foster care until the most wonderful couple I've ever known adopted me. The reasons I went into law enforcement, why I became an expert in biological weapons and why I drink coffee every day are all the same." She took a deeper breath this time. She'd never admitted what she said next to anyone. Not even her adoptive parents or Alana.

Noah let her take her moment, attentive and solemn.

"I do everything I do to remember and honor my mother. I try to help people and find justice for those who couldn't, I became an expert in an awful subject to try to keep people safe from it, and I remind myself with every cup of coffee that you shouldn't stop trying to love life just because there are people out there who only want to destroy it."

There it was.

She'd given her most-guarded secret to a man she'd only known a week.

Noah's expression was impassive. She'd had no idea how he would react since she'd never told anyone about her parents before.

He must have realized that.

"Why did you tell me this?"

The truth wasn't done with Carly yet. So she gave it to him straight.

"You just feel right."

Whatever the answer he was searching for, that seemed to do the trick.

Noah took her chin in his hands and dipped low for a kiss so tantalizing that Carly nearly went weak in the knees. Warm was the best way to describe Noah, followed by solid. He was a force. A quiet strength that reached out to every part of her body. That strength moved from his hands to his tongue as it swept across her lips and deepened their kiss.

It felt absolutely right.

Carly made a noise against him, unable to hide her pleasure at the move. He reciprocated the feeling by wrapping an arm around her and pulling her flush against his body. They stayed like that for a few moments, enjoying the tight and rhythmic embrace.

Until they wanted more.

Noah took a step back, lips swollen and red. His eyes betrayed him as they listed in the direction of the bedroom.

Carly, filled with heat that went from below her waistline all the way to her cheeks, found herself grinning.

Noah seemed a little uncertain.

Had she gone too fast in an already accelerated timeline?

"I can't offer you champagne or walks along the beach right now, and I can't offer you beers and dive bars, either," Noah said. "But I *can* do my best to show you a good time, if you want it."

If Carly hadn't been ready before, she sure was now.

In answer, she took his hand.

Then she led him to the bedroom.

SUNLIGHT POURED IN through the curtains and warmed the side of Noah's face. It took him a few seconds to realize what that meant.

He'd slept past the sunrise.

Something he hadn't done in a long time.

Normally that would have started his day off with

an uneasiness. Like he'd already wasted the morning by sleeping through it.

Not today.

The reason he was still in bed was in part from an exhausting few days, but mostly because of what he'd been doing in the time between the sheets leading up to falling asleep.

He'd been afraid to touch Carly for fear of hurting her or reopening any of her wounds. Carly, however, had not shared that fear. They'd split the difference of concern for a night filled with passion, care and heat.

Now Noah awoke feeling good.

Feeling…right.

The bed dipped down a little next to him. He rolled over to find Carly looked as guilty as sin and just as delicious. Her golden hair caught the morning light while his shirt engulfed her upper body. Her legs were bare, and she'd brought a plate of cookies to bed with her. She looked apologetic.

"I was going to eat these in the kitchen but then I got nervous that Gina or your dad would walk in and see me without pants and with obvious bedhead *so* I brought these in here but then I was cold so…" She held up one of the cookies he'd made her the night before. "I'm sorry for bringing cookies into your bed."

Noah laughed. A real, genuine belly laugh. He propped himself up against the headboard and swiped one of the cookies.

"Just for future reference, cookies in bed? Something you never have to apologize for." To prove his point, he took a huge bite of his own tree-shaped cookie. Unlike the mostly from-scratch stew recipe he'd begun the night before, these were the easy fifteen-minute frozen kind of cookie. But boy, they tasted good.

Or maybe it was the company that made them taste like a piece of heaven.

Carly laughed but nodded. She took a bite of her cookie as she slipped her legs back under the sheets. On reflex, Noah moved his free hand to rest on her thigh.

It pulled a quick smile from the woman.

Then her brow creased.

"What's wrong?" he asked, instantly worried. After they'd finished their nighttime activities they'd spent some time in the shower together. Then, Noah had been careful to re-dress her cuts. "Are you feeling okay?"

Carly sighed but nodded.

"Yeah. I feel fine. I mean, I feel sore and some things still sting, but it's not bad. I think sleep really helped."

"Then what's on your mind?"

Carly took another bite of cookie. As she chewed, she looked like she was working through answering that herself.

"I guess I just keep coming back to the chair," she finally said.

"The chair?"

Carly readjusted so she was facing him. He moved her legs so there was room for them to lie across his lap. She might have been half-naked in his bed, eating a plate of Christmas cookies, but in that moment Carly Welsh looked every bit the FBI agent working a case.

"The chair in David Lapp's basement. It doesn't make sense."

"How so? Rodney Lee sure seemed like a man who wouldn't mind trying to torture someone."

"See, *that* part makes sense from what we know of him. Rodney was obsessive and abusive and seemed to be prone to impulse and aggression. But bolting a chair to the floor in someone's basement and putting restraints on it? I mean, I get him trying to muscle information out of David and needing a way to keep him from escaping, but the chair just screams premeditation. *Thought.* Finesse." She looked down at her wrists. There was some rope burn around them. Noah had put some ointment on them before they'd gone to bed. He'd had to hide how angry it had made him to see and feel physical evidence of how close Carly had come to dying. Even now it made his blood pressure rise.

"But the setup in the barn had the same feel," she countered herself. "It was *theatrical.* Like tying someone to the train tracks, when shooting them would be so much faster *and* easier."

"But shooting someone doesn't make a statement. At least, not like what I saw in that barn."

"That's what I also don't get," she hurried to say. "Rodney Lee, as far as we know, has been all about finding Talia. What statement was he trying to make? And to whom? My team? 'Hey, I'm a guy with a seemingly endless supply of anthrax who can derail an investigation by killing a federal agent.'" She shook her head. "And *that's* one more thing that's really bothering me."

She put the cookie in her hand down, completely focused.

"One *really* good way to not have the FBI, or any

law enforcement, crawling around town here in the first place is to *not* spread fields' worth of anthrax randomly. And certainly not send a tape of you kidnapping a guy to his mother to use as leverage against her *to then use* to get her to help kill the FBI agent you brought to town in the first place!"

Carly let out a frustrated breath.

"I have to admit, when you put it like that it sounds like Rodney wasn't the sharpest tool in the shed."

"When I put it like that he doesn't even sound like the sharpest tool in the superstore. I mean, I've had cases where not every loose thread is tied up, but this? It feels like it's reverted back into a ball of yarn."

"Maybe the team found something last night. Weren't they all waiting on one thing or the other?"

"I'm waiting on an update from them." She averted her gaze to the half-eaten cookie. She wasn't done with the ball of yarn yet. "David and Talia have to still be here, right? There had to be some reason Rodney was sticking around."

Her tone turned thoughtful. It matched her gaze as it moved to his.

"Why did *you* stay?"

"Why did I stay?" It was a question he'd heard over and over again, yet one he'd never answered. For a while that had been because there was no one he *wanted* to know the answer, but now?

Hadn't Carly just shared her past with him? Hadn't she let down her guard and let him in? Could he do the same?

Did he *want* to?

Yellow house, Noah. The dream for your life. Why you walked away. The freedom and peace you wanted. You already thought it once.

Carly's brows pulled together. Her face fell a little.

She knew he was debating telling her and it hurt.

Noah opened his mouth, to say what he wasn't sure, but her phone on the bed next to them blared to life.

The moment was over.

Carly put the plate down and pulled her legs off of him. When she answered her phone, she was all business.

"What's going on, Max?"

Noah couldn't hear what the agent said but, judging by Carly's expression, it was a bombshell. She flung herself out of the bed and started moving around to find her clothes. He followed suit, trying to pick up on the conversation, but could only catch a few words here and there.

It wasn't until he was dressed that Carly ended the call and found him in the kitchen.

"Rodney Lee didn't make sense because he wasn't the one pulling the strings," she nearly sang. "He had a partner."

Chapter Nineteen

"Dylan, adult son of real estate developer Caroline Ferry, never checked into the rehab facility in Florida."

Aria was using the rental SUV to block the cold wind that had picked up since Carly and Noah had arrived at the Ferry Mansion. She had her bulletproof vest on and badge pinned to it. She looked like a woman not to be tested. Small was the package, but mighty was the strength.

"The team is inside sweeping the place, but Dylan isn't here. But we *do* have several updates for you," Aria continued. "Headquarters did a lot of the work on this one. Opaline finally got the info from the rehab facility, and Amanda and Alana were able to spot the van from the casino cameras with the same plates we were looking for leaving *and* going back to the parking garage. Opaline couldn't get a good shot of his face, but Rodney was seen both times leaving through the lobby right after. Not the smartest crayon in the box."

Noah next to them smirked.

"Not the sharpest tool in the superstore, either."

Carly snorted, then asked the most obvious question she could think of.

"How do we prove that Dylan connects with Rodney?"

Just because Dylan seemed like a perfect fit for the crime—motive, means and missing alibi—didn't mean he was guilty of it.

Aria was ready with an answer. A nice change of pace for the case.

"Well, Axel started thinking that, if Dylan was in town, there was a good chance he'd been going to the casino and maybe that was how he met Rodney." Aria pulled her phone out and went to the photo gallery app. When she found the picture she wanted, she held it up. "Amanda starting matching posts Rodney was tagged in on social media by Rob Cantos to security footage from around the same time at the casino. She got a hit from two months ago."

The picture was of two men standing outside of the casino's front sidewalk talking and smoking.

"That's Rodney," Carly confirmed, pointing to the man on the left.

Aria pointed to the man on the right.

"And that's Dylan. When he was supposed to be in rehab." She took her phone back but kept on. "Max ran with the info and went to the floor of the casino to start asking around using the photo. Turns out not only were both men regulars, they were *regularly* seen together for the last six months. Right around the time that the deal with his mother fell through is when their friendship seemed to start."

"So they definitely know each other," Noah said. "What did Dylan's mother have to say?"

Both Carly and Aria turned to him, surprised.

"Sorry, I didn't mean to overstep. You're the agents."

Carly shook her head.

"No apology necessary." She gave him a look that perhaps wasn't smart to share in front of Aria. It felt smoldering, but Carly couldn't help it.

Noah as a detective was an interesting, and stimulating, thought.

Aria smiled wide and bounced her gaze between them. Suspicious, and then somewhat excited.

Thankfully, she didn't say what she was thinking and, instead, answered his question.

"Caroline had no idea that he wasn't in rehab and when we told her the first thing she did was call her accountant. Turns out she's missing money, much to her second surprise."

"How much are we talking?"

"According to Alana, more than enough to procure a ridiculous amount of anthrax powder on the black market if you knew the right people."

Carly raised her eyebrow at that.

"And Ms. Ferry didn't notice that much money missing?"

Aria lowered her voice even though they were out in the drive.

"You know how we thought that she was really rich before? Triple that number in your head and you're in the ballpark."

"So a large amount of money draining from one of

her accounts isn't going to pop up on her radar for a while, since she already has more than that," Carly finished.

Aria made a finger gun.

"Bingo."

"But, because of the seriousness of the case, Rihanna was able to get us a warrant before we knew any of this?"

A lot had happened while Carly had been sleeping. If she didn't trust her team, that would have made her skin crawl. Missing out on helping to solve the case already had Carly fighting a feeling of anxiousness. Though even she had to admit that she'd needed to take a temporary back seat after running into Rodney Lee twice.

"Yep," Aria answered. "And since then the evidence is going from circumstantial to in the direction of damning. Wanna guess what we just found in the Ferry wine cellar?"

Carly didn't try. She was nearly vibrating in anticipation.

Answers were starting to feel as good as Noah had the night before.

Almost.

"Hit me," she said.

Aria didn't disappoint.

"A bolt gun with no bolts and fibers in a package that used to hold rope. CSI will have to compare it to the rope in David's basement and the one used on you but—"

Carly interrupted with a rush of adrenaline.

"It's too much of a coincidence not to be a match."

Carly turned to Noah. "That's why it was bothering me. Dylan was the one who set up the chair and the trap in the barn, not Rodney."

He smiled, almost like he was proud.

It was oddly satisfying.

Aria continued with their expert profiler's opinion.

"Axel said based on what he's seen and read on Dylan, he's a lot craftier, a lot smarter and has a lot more anger in him than we originally thought. He thinks losing the dude ranch deal might have made Dylan snap and that we're looking at a man who wants to punish those who he thinks have wronged him. Not to intimidate or use it as an opportunity to get the deal going again."

"Poisoning the community is a slow, malicious way to do damage and savor the fallout," Carly hated to say. "It's definitely a longer-lasting punishment."

She thought of her father.

Noah's jaw clenched. So did his fist at his side next to her.

"How does Rodney fit into that plan then?" he asked after a beat.

Now that Carly knew there were two suspects and not just one, she was putting together a theory in record time.

"If Opaline had not kept digging into his rehab, we might not have looked twice at Dylan past our initial contact. Everything else that we had on Rodney was enough to close the case, even with loose threads. Rodney attacked and tried to kill me twice, the second time with anthrax, admitted he had connections to get it, and

might have had an ax to grind with the Amish community thanks to his hatred of David. You said it yourself,
though, Dylan was craftier and smarter than Rodney,
and we all know that Rodney is obsessed with Talia to
the point where I bet if he was offered a way to find
her, he'd do almost anything."

"So you think Dylan used Rodney for his connections and then was planning on letting him take the
fall," Noah spelled out.

Carly nodded.

"If you're determined to follow through on something you know is going to pull severe heat from the
law, then you're going to want to make sure someone
else gets burned. Not you."

Noah conceded to that.

"Regardless of the motive and the partnership, we
still have one problem." Aria shook her head. "Dylan
isn't here and we can't find him. Caroline froze all of
his accounts still connected with hers so if he needs
money to run then he'll need that to be cash, which
won't make things easy."

Carly put her hands on her hips and bit at her bottom lip.

"Why didn't he run before?" she asked after a moment.

"He wanted to see the suffering he'd inflicted?"
Noah tried.

"But he had a pretty decent alibi until Opaline took
a look at it. Why not leave when things started heat-
ing up? Why— Oh my God!" Carly felt her eyes go as

wide as quarters. Noah and Aria both went on the defensive, startled.

Carly didn't have time to apologize.

Another piece of the puzzle fell in place.

"At the barn, Willa seemed focused solely on doing Rodney's bidding, but it was Dylan pulling the strings," Carly continued. "Even if she knew that, it didn't matter. All that mattered was her family's safety."

Carly looked up at the massive house. Then around them at the land and trees. Noah picked up on her thoughts.

"Willa wouldn't forsake her beliefs unless she had proof that her family was in danger," he said. "And she'd need more than one video on a phone, I'd think, to serve someone up to be killed."

Carly felt the same way.

"We know that Dylan set up the chair in David's basement... What if David never escaped from that chair? What if Dylan decided to use him as a way to gain leverage over a local? A mother who would be hesitant to talk to the cops, even under normal circumstances, would make a great lackey to help him stay ahead of us and out of the spotlight."

Aria understood where they were going, too, and chimed in.

"Dylan punishes the town that he thinks ruined him. He gets Rodney's help because of his connections, to poison it. Then he makes a plan to pin it all on Rodney by using David, the one person Rodney hates the most, as a way to control him."

"All while using the one person who loves David

the most to play the other side," Carly finished. They shared a look with one another.

"It's all conjecture still," Aria said, playing the devil's advocate.

Carly agreed…with caveats.

"But I can tell you with confidence that my gut is saying Dylan has to have David stashed somewhere. Have you searched *all* of the property?"

Aria opened her mouth to answer, literally forming the word across her lips, when life decided to flex its muscles.

Life was often about timing.

And now was a great example of that.

Selena hustled out of the house, catching their attention. Max was quick on her heels. Blanca was in front of both.

Aria went on full alert. Carly did, too.

Then Axel rounded the team out hurrying outside. His attention went to them and he didn't stop moving as he spoke.

"We were looking through the property's security system and saw a woman crawling in the grass by the side gate."

No more needed to be said.

Carly followed behind her team while Noah came after her as everyone converged on the area they'd seen from the footage.

Selena and Blanca got there first, but it was Max who called out for an ambulance. Aria saw the woman and pivoted to make sure one was on its way, while Axel dropped down to start working on her. Carly lowered herself next to the woman and did a quick scan of her wounds.

Her knuckles were busted and her dress was stained with dirt and blood. She had rolled over from her side to her back, giving them an easy view to the gunshot wound at her side.

But she was alive and conscious.

She was also Willa Lapp.

When she saw Carly, relief as plain as day spread across her expression.

"You're okay."

Her voice was tired, weak. Carly looked back at the path the woman had crawled along. It led into the woods.

"Where are you coming from?" Carly asked, diving right in. "And who did this to you?"

Willa cried out as Axel put pressure on the gunshot wound. Tears sprang up at the corners of her eyes, but she answered.

And what an answer it was.

"There's an old maintenance work building that way." She pointed with a shaking hand toward the trees. "He—he tried to take him so I tried to stop him."

"Who did you try to stop? Who shot you?" Carly echoed the question that everyone was hoping they knew the answer to.

"Dylan."

When Willa said his name, excitement surged through Carly. They were closer to their goal. Justice.

Willa didn't know it, but she'd found this case's magic word for the team.

"Spread out," Carly ordered but everyone was already moving.

Aria switched places with Axel, gun out, while the rest of the Tactical Crime Division team moved into and through the trees.

Noah even tagged along but kept behind them, quiet and on alert.

It wasn't until they came up to a small building, rundown and looking like it had been forgotten by the world, that Carly asked him to stay put.

He obliged with a whisper.

"Be careful."

Carly nodded. Then it was all about the building.

Small but sturdy. They took no chances as they entered and then methodically cleared the rooms.

What they contained sickened her.

One room made the hair on the back of Carly's neck stand. Axel swore. Selena did, too.

A long table housed a bank of monitors. Each of those monitors displayed a view into the Castle in the Trees Inn. More specifically, into their individual rooms.

If that was all they had found, that would have been enough.

Yet, the next room is what got to Carly the most.

She met the young man, bloodied and bruised but alive, in the middle of the room, tied to a chair and gagged. They quickly untethered him, and he stood, swaying.

"I sure am glad to finally meet you, David," Carly said.

David Lapp collapsed against Max, understandably exhausted.

"We need to get him and his mother to hospital ASAP," Carly started. "Then we—"

She didn't get to finish.

Noah burst into the room with eyes that were crazed and his cell phone clutched in his hand.

Something was wrong.

Something was really wrong.

Ice filled her veins before he could even get the words out.

"Gina called. My dad and brother Thomas came by the house." His nostrils flared in anger but his eyes yelled worry. "And Dylan just showed up there now."

He shook his head. It hurt him to say what he did next.

"He took Thomas. He took my little brother."

Chapter Twenty

It was Christmas Eve and Noah was finally spending it with his family. Every member but one.

Noah's mother, Marta, hadn't moved an inch since she'd come out to the blockade made up of SUVs and Noah's and Gina's trucks. Local PD was also there but had been told to make a perimeter around the Yoders' property while they surveyed the barn.

The barn where it had all started.

The barn where Noah's little brother was being held hostage by a desperate man with, according to him, nothing to lose.

Noah's father was less stationary than his mother. He paced a small lane between the vehicles while the Tactical Crime Division team did their recon and made their plan.

Noah wanted to help, but trusted Carly and her team to do their job.

Something he kept having to reiterate to his father.

"She can do it. *They* can do it," he said again. "I know it doesn't mean much to you, but I trust them."

That had finally gotten his mother moving. She

turned around, dark hair and green eyes an identical match to his, and walked to his side.

Noah didn't know what to do for a moment. Or, more aptly, didn't know how to feel.

While his father had made the decision to label him as an outsider after he left, Noah's mother hadn't originally been happy with the decision. She'd been vocal about them still talking to and having him come over, yet that hadn't lasted past the first month that he'd left.

Now he was caught between them and worried for a brother he barely knew.

"I don't know them," his father said, words dangerously close to sounding disgusted. "And I don't know her."

That was it.

That was enough.

It wasn't the time, certainly not the place, but an anger and hurt that Noah didn't realize was still there came to the surface with startling speed.

"You don't know *me*, and yet I'm who you call when there's trouble. Sometimes life isn't fair like that and you just have to put your faith in someone other than yourself."

He hadn't meant to say it, and not with the amount of bite he had, and yet he still wanted to say more.

So he did.

"I have known Carly for a week and she and her team have shown more compassion, caring and dedication to helping this town than most people who live here. They have risked their lives and almost paid with them to protect all of us and do you know what they get in return?" Noah pointed to himself. "A liaison, because you wouldn't even *talk* to them."

Noah shook his head. Then motioned to the group a few yards ahead of them with a different barricade they'd created themselves. Carly had her bulletproof vest on and gun at her side. Noah hated that he couldn't be next to her, that he couldn't go inside that barn to rescue his brother with her, that he couldn't guarantee her safety.

So he let his feeling of helplessness pull out the rest of his hurt at his family forsaking him.

"I just want you to remember that all of the people who you ignore with such disdain are the same people who you call in your darkest hours. So to stand here and look down at any of them, at *me*, doesn't help anyone. Not an inch."

Noah's father had stopped his pacing. His mother has gone still.

Noah could have said more, but he knew it wouldn't do any good. At the end of the day, no matter his age, when he was around his parents he felt like a little kid who'd taken a left at the fork in the road instead of their right. A boy who had felt lost for years going along his path alone.

That is, until he found a yellow house, a blue shed and a home along the way.

The Tucketts.

Gina, who had not only tried to fend off Dylan, narrowly missing getting shot herself, had also taken off in her truck to chase the man until he bailed out into the closest building he'd been near. She and her family had never been fans of people in general, but they'd given him the space to decide if he wanted to be one of the few they did consider to be good.

And it was only now, standing there next to his flesh and blood, that Noah realized Gina's father hadn't given him the farm.

Noah had inherited it like a son would from a father.

Because he *was* family.

And, even though it had taken him this long to realize he hadn't been truly alone all of these years, he found the sudden clarity deflated the same anger that had brought it on.

His parents *were* good people. People who had spent their lives dedicated to their beliefs. Just as he wanted them to not fault him for the path he'd taken away from them, Noah couldn't fault them for staying on the path they'd been walking their whole lives.

Noah let out a long breath.

Then he looked between his parents and meant what he said next.

"I'm sorry. I just miss you sometimes."

A hand, small and worn, took his. Noah's mother wasn't smiling, but she squeezed his hand.

"And we miss you always. Don't you ever think otherwise."

Noah didn't know what to say to that, so he didn't say a thing. He held his mother's hand while his father looked conflicted.

Finally he let out his own breath before gazing out at the barn in the distance.

"When this is over maybe it's time we start to fix that." He turned back to Noah. "I could always use an extra pair of hands to help mend fences."

It wasn't what Noah had expected, but he took his father's olive branch all the same.

"I've gotten really good at those over the last few years."

They all shared a silence, the first one since he'd left as a teenager that wasn't filled with confusion, disappointment and resentment.

It felt nice.

But it didn't last long.

Something was happening with the TCD team.

They were splitting up. Axel went one way, Selena the other, while the rest spread out along their barricade, guns drawn.

All except Carly.

She gave her weapon over to Aria and then held her hands up in surrender.

Then she walked out into the open field.

And right into the barn.

THOMAS MILLER LOOKED like a younger version of Noah. So much so that, had they not known whom Dylan had taken, Carly would have figured it out the moment she saw him.

Even afraid and held against a desperate man without an exit strategy, a solid strength emanated out of how he held himself. Never mind his forest green eyes.

"I'm unarmed and alone," Carly called out, hands still up for emphasis. "So let's talk about this."

Dylan had seen better days.

Unlike his mother, who had been the picture of cool elegance, it was obvious he was hanging on by a thread.

The suit he wore was torn and covered in dirt. He had angry red marks with dried blood along the side of his face, courtesy of Willa Lapp she presumed, and he was sweating despite the cold.

However, the hand that held the gun pressed into Thomas's side was steady.

So was his voice.

"Stop right there," he demanded.

They were standing against the far wall of the barn. It was smaller than the abandoned one on the Kellogg property.

Which was good, but also not so good.

Carly could see all the exits as soon as she was inside. So could Dylan and, with his back against the only wall without one, that meant no surprises.

For either of them.

The main reason why the rest of the team was hanging back.

That and their belief that Dylan had already snapped once, so every complication to his plan after was just that break splintering even more. If he felt like there was no way out, he'd shoot Thomas.

And Carly wasn't going to let that happen. He'd tried to kill her, using Rodney. It had been an easy choice for her, to be the one to step up to try to get Thomas back. She wanted to face this man.

"Let's just calm down here," Carly said, stopping a

few yards from him. "Your best option for this to turn out in your favor is to let him go and come with me."

Dylan didn't waste any time.

"Did you find David and Willa?"

Carly struggled to keep her expression impassive on that one.

"We did."

He didn't seem upset, which put Carly further on edge.

"Did you find Aaron?"

This time she wasn't able to hide her reaction. He actually grinned.

"See, I've been to enough support groups to know the best motivation usually comes from wanting what's best for your family. That's why I didn't just stop with Willa."

"You got her youngest son, too."

"Yep. And right now he's in an undisclosed, yet very public place, with two bags of anthrax and a cell phone." He nodded down to his jacket. "And, unless he gets a call from me in the next—" He glanced quickly at his watch. It, like the suit, looked expensive and yet wrong with his desperation. "—seven minutes, he's going to release that powder into a ventilation system… One that feeds into a wing of, drumroll please, the hospital. Which, I don't have to tell you, our resident biological weapons expert, anthrax plus hospital patients can't be a good combination."

Carly was stunned.

Absolutely stunned.

"Aaron doesn't know we found his mother and

brother," she realized. "You threatened them if he didn't do this, didn't you?"

Dylan's grin turned malicious.

"You get the mother to help by threatening the son, and you get the other son to help by threatening the mother. It's the circle of life."

Carly's gears were spinning fast.

She didn't know Aaron Lapp, but his mother had almost gotten Carly killed to keep David safe. She had no doubt that Aaron would do the same for his mother.

"This place is surrounded. You can't get away," she said, changing subjects. "But if you let Thomas go and call off Aaron I'll make sure to let everyone know that you cooperated."

It was a shot in the dark, appealing to the rational side of the man holding a gun to a teenager's side.

Dylan didn't bite.

"I cooperated? Those are just words, Agent Welsh. We both know that if I get taken in that will be the end of me."

"You didn't kill anyone," she tried again. "That counts for something."

"But I orchestrated everything."

There it was.

His own admission.

Yet, she still didn't know *why*.

So she asked.

"Why, though? Why go through all of this trouble in the first place? To punish the community?"

Dylan's expression went hard.

Angry.

"Because one day everything was fine and the next I was out of money, out of my house and being sent to another place ready to tell me I needed to stop what I loved doing." He was seething. "Meeting Rodney just opened up a world of possibilities on how to finally have a win I could keep."

That's what it was.

That was who *he* was.

Standing there Carly finally saw it, clear as day.

Dylan wasn't a punisher. He was a seeker of justice. Too bad it was the wrong kind.

"You wanted to use what the community loved against them, just like you used what Rodney and the Lapps loved most against them." She looked at Thomas. "Just like you're using Thomas against me, because of Noah."

His anger transformed into another awful, no-good grin.

"We've been watching you since you got here, Agent Welsh. It's been easy to see that the fastest way to get the team to pay attention is go for their lead agent. And since Rodney failed, *twice* at that, I realized an attack against your farmer would be the next best way." He jabbed the gun into Thomas's side. "Now, you're going to go out there and tell them all to stand down and let me leave or, not only is Thomas here going to die, but somewhere out there a hospital is about to be in a really bad way."

Carly wanted to keep talking, wanted to get to know

the mind behind the senseless and selfish acts of violence and destruction, but the truth was, sometimes the bad guy was one-dimensional. Sometimes they didn't make sense. Some didn't know why they did what they did, and others refused to ever say.

No one knew exactly why Carly's father had poisoned her mother. She probably never would. It was a fact that she'd struggled with since she was ten and would most likely still struggle with until it was her time to go into the great beyond.

But there were just some things you had to learn to accept or they'd eat you up.

Dylan, for whatever reason, had taken the curveball thrown at him and, instead of hitting it, had decided to blow up the stadium.

And Carly was going to have to accept that she would never fully understand why.

So there were no more questions left to ask of the case, of the man.

They had their answers.

Now it was time for the wrap-up.

"Did you get all of that?" Carly put her hand to her ear. Axel's voice came through the earpiece in a concise answer.

"Yes. We'll stand down. But, Carly? He's not going to make that call, even if we let him go. You need to get Thomas away from him before he gets into that car."

Carly nodded to Dylan. He snorted, unaware of the Plan B the TCD team had already accounted for.

"You've been on comms the entire time. Just like in the movies. That's clever."

"More like efficient," she said. "They've agreed to all stand down. The car you came in is still outside. You're free to go to it, *after* you give us Thomas and make the call."

She knew it was a no-go, but she had to make the effort.

Dylan shook his head.

"He comes with me to the car, then I'll call when I'm far enough away." He flipped his watch back and shook his head again. "Take it or leave it, because now we're down to three minutes."

"Fine, but if you hurt him, the deal is off."

"Deal. Now go ahead of us."

Carly put her hands back up and led Dylan and Thomas out. She had to hand it to the boy, he was quiet and calm. He definitely was a Miller.

The world outside the barn was quiet. Local PD had the perimeter, but to her left she saw her team and then she saw Noah and his parents.

Everyone was watching her.

Then all eyes were on Dylan.

Carly turned around to face him and the car that was parked at the corner of the building.

"Now let him go," she said, voice low.

Dylan's flare of confidence was starting to fray. His eyes were wide as he looked at his audience. The firm grip he'd had on the gun was wavering.

All she needed was one opening.

"Dylan. Let him go."

That's when she heard it.

Small, scared and set in his own plan.

He'd done the math.

He'd used all of the aces up his sleeve.

He wasn't going to make it far, if he made it out at all. "No."

He readjusted the gun and that's when the world was destined to become loud and chaotic.

Thomas might have been young, but he wasn't defenseless. He threw his weight forward just as Carly lunged at him. Dylan stumbled at the shift and gave Carly her only opening.

She met Thomas in the middle, grabbed his arms and used his momentum to spin him around so his back was to his family.

Just in time for her to see Noah over his shoulder as Dylan shot her in the back.

The force of the hit sent Carly and Thomas to the ground just as the yelling started. Then the gun shots over them.

Carly couldn't breathe, but she stayed on top of the boy as a shield while her team used their firepower to cover them.

The sound of a car starting preceded the screeching of tires a few moments later.

Thomas opened his eyes.

Forest green. Just like his brother's.

"Carly!"

The edge of her vision started to go black.

Someone walked past her, calm and cool.

Max.

Their Plan B.

She heard the shot he must have taken. Then the car crash.

Then she heard Noah.

But she couldn't stay awake for him.

Chapter Twenty-One

Noah spent Christmas morning making cookies. He made reindeer-shaped ones, though they didn't look that great. Selena told him it didn't matter as long as the icing was done well.

So she took over that job, while Blanca chewed on a dog bone in front of the Christmas tree.

While the rest of the team had gone back to the inn after a busy night, she'd accepted Noah's offer for the guest bedroom.

She hadn't wanted to leave her friend and, after seeing what he had yesterday, he understood.

Carly being shot was something he absolutely never wanted to see again.

"I was going to say I don't mind how they look, I'll eat the cookies, but then I heard frosting, so I'm inclined to agree with Selena."

The woman of the hour walked slowly into the kitchen. She'd changed out of his T-shirt and into a simple red dress with boots. Noah couldn't help but stare.

She laughed, then winced.

"I brought one good holiday-worthy outfit, just in

case the holiday spirit found me. But, let me tell you, this look starts and stops with the dress." She slid carefully onto a barstool across from them. "It hurts to breathe so I'm not about to do my hair or make-up."

Noah frowned, remembering the moment she'd been shot.

After Carly had used herself as a human shield for his brother, he had felt like he couldn't breathe, either. He'd started running for her before Max ever took his one shot that ended Dylan's luck.

When she'd gone slack before he could get to her?

Breathing became the least of his worries.

But then he'd seen the bulletproof vest beneath her jacket.

It was only after they'd been discharged from the hospital with a few bruised ribs on her left side that he'd started breathing normally again.

"You were shot *yesterday*," Selena reminded her. "I would still be in my PJs and asleep if I were you."

Carly laughed then winced again.

"The smell of cookies and coffee is a surprisingly strong motivator. Speaking of—" Carly turned to Noah, an expression he couldn't read moved across her face. Then softened. "Do you mind making me a cup?"

It was such a simple request, but Noah knew now what it meant to ask.

It only cemented his plans for the yellow house on the hill.

"It would be my pleasure."

He went to the coffee maker and started as Selena

updated Carly on everything she'd missed while she'd been in the hospital and then sleeping in his bed.

"Aria said that Dylan is out of surgery and should make a full recovery. The doctor actually complimented Max on the precision of the shot. It was enough to get him to wreck but didn't kill him." Selena snorted. "Max said he'd never gotten complimented from a doctor before about shooting someone."

"Hey, given he did it while walking through a field while Dylan was in a car speeding away? Max deserves all the praise as far as I'm concerned."

"True dat." Selena passed Noah a finished cookie while he went for a mug in the cabinet. Carly already had one in front of her, a bite missing, in the small window of time he'd turned his back to them.

It made him happy.

"And what about Aaron?" she asked after giving him a little smile. "Did he tell us anything we didn't know?"

After Max had taken the doctor-praised shot, he'd gone ahead and grabbed Dylan's phone and dialed the most recent call in the phone's log.

Aaron had answered, but hadn't believed Max until Noah's brother, Aaron's best friend, had told him that it was over.

In fact, his mother, Willa, had just been admitted into the same hospital.

Aaron had cooperated 100 percent after that. He'd stayed with the still-sealed bags of anthrax until hazmat had arrived.

They'd been the ones to discover that the bags contained flour, not anthrax.

Apparently Dylan's seemingly endless supply had had an end.

Selena nodded.

"Well, more of 'filled in some blanks.' You know the creepy surveillance room? Apparently he was the one forced to install the cameras at the inn when we were out in the field and then his job was to watch them to see if there was anything Dylan could use to stay ahead of us. He was told if he didn't do it then it was the same as killing his mother and brother. Pretty heavy for a fifteen-year-old who's never really seen violence."

"That'd be pretty heavy to me, too," Noah commented. Both women agreed.

Then Carly was all about the threads she'd been trying to weave together since they found the chair in the basement.

"Has David woken up yet?"

Selena clapped her hands, just as Carly had done the day before in excitement at remembering something.

"I meant for this to be my first bit of news to you but I got sidetracked by the cookies! Not only did David Lapp wake up, he became one of my favorite heroes." Noah had finished making the coffee and came around the breakfast bar and took the seat next to Carly, also curious. Noah had missed out on a lot of what happened since he'd been with Carly from the moment the ambulance took her from the barn.

"Turns out he met Talia in the city when he had to go in to get supplies for his father. He said it was *lightning*. Love at first sight. When he found out she was trapped in an abusive relationship with an older man who was clearly obsessed with her, he brought her to his family's house and hid her the best he could. *But* when his father confronted him about how sketchy he'd been acting, he was afraid if he told the truth that word would spread and Rodney would find her."

"So he let himself be kicked out of the community to keep her secret," Noah said, already impressed by David's compassion.

She nodded.

"Yep. She gave him the money to help rent the house and stayed there with him. Their plan was to save more money and leave town, but then Dylan grabbed him. David said he woke up in his own basement and in front of a very angry Rodney Lee." A flash of anger burned through Selena's words. "He effectively tortured David, trying to find out where Talia had gone. But that boy refused to give her up. Then, when Rodney left, that's when Dylan came back for him and took him out to the Ferry estate where he treated him like a prisoner and motivation for Willa to help Dylan. He also said that, he wasn't sure, but he thought Dylan kept feeding Rodney fake information about seeing or hearing of David around town. That's why we think Rodney stayed after he disappeared."

Carly wrapped her hand around the coffee mug. When she took a sip, Noah couldn't help but smile a little.

"Where was Talia? Was she not at David's house?"

"Get this. David was so worried about her that they came up with a safe place for her to go if she ever felt unsafe or something happened. A place that she'd be safe until he could come get her. She went there when she saw Rodney in town and had no idea David had been taken. Once she realized something was wrong, David was already missing, so she went back to wait to see if he showed up. Guess where that safe place was?"

Selena leaned in and actually cackled.

Noah was leaning in, too.

"Where?" he asked, completely invested.

"We have *no* idea."

"What?" Carly asked around a mouthful of coffee.

Selena laughed and straightened.

"Once the news broke yesterday afternoon, Talia Jones showed up at the foot of David's hospital bed late last night and hasn't left since. Aria said that Talia was the first person David saw when he woke up. They wouldn't tell us where she'd been and since the case is closed, we didn't care to keep asking." She touched her chest and made a dramatic sigh. "I know I don't know them but, damn, what a love story. I hope they make it."

Noah's father, who had asked Gina to take him to the hospital to personally thank Carly and the team, had already given him a piece of gossip that he didn't think the other two knew yet. Apparently, during their limited interactions in his captivity, David had told his mother that he loved Talia with all of his heart and planned to marry her when it was all over. Willa had in turn told her husband who had, in turn, reached out to Noah's father.

"He asked me advice on how to deal with a child who chooses to leave," his father had said.

"And what did you say?"

His father, a devout man who was as quiet as he was stubborn, had softened. It hadn't been a lot, but enough to notice.

"I told him he should learn to accept that we all walk our own paths and that's not always a bad thing. Just different."

He'd clapped Noah on the shoulder after that and then Gina had taken him home.

It wasn't a brand-new beginning for them, but it wasn't an ending, either.

Now Carly turned to him.

"Do you think he'll try to go back since he left under extraordinary circumstances?"

Noah was quick to answer.

"No. I think he's going to stick with his lightning, his love."

At that, she smiled.

The rest of the conversation bounced back and forth between the more technical details of what happened next and, Carly cringed as she said it, paperwork. They ate cookies and welcomed Gina. She was the beginning of a long line of guests, including the entire TCD team and Noah's staff. The morning turned to afternoon and, for the first time since he owned the farm, the house was filled with talking, laughter and actual cheer.

Christmas day at his house came and went. Those who couldn't get out to their families video-chatted and made promises to see them the next day, while Alana and Opaline joined in through FaceTime.

Before dessert was ready, Noah felt it was time to finally tell Carly the truth.

And ask her a question he never thought he'd ask anyone.

After making sure she felt up for it, he drove her to a part of the property she hadn't yet seen.

"Too much holiday spirit and needed a break?" she teased him after he set her up on the tailgate of the truck.

He laughed and sat next to her.

"It was just enough to show me I wouldn't mind something like this every year."

Carly smiled.

She was beautiful.

"I have to admit, it's turning me around on the whole holiday season."

He wanted to keep bantering with her, but knew it was now or never.

Noah let every wall he had down and finally told someone the truth.

"It was a yellow house."

"A yellow house?" Her tone had gone soft. She'd caught on to the change in him. He'd known her a week and she could read him better than anyone he knew.

He nodded and pointed in the distance. There was nothing but open field and sky.

"There used to be a yellow house there, owned by the Tucketts, until it burned down about ten years ago. It was originally for the full-time staff but had been empty for twenty years before that. The first time I saw it, I was twelve. I was crossing through the farm to go home after sneaking out to fish." He let out a breath and shook his head, still unable to understand why the feeling that had followed next had happened. "One second I was a kid without any doubts in my future and then, the moment after I saw that house, everything changed. I wanted more. I wanted different.

"Then I left on Rumspringa and never went back home," he continued. "I was lucky enough to find a place on the farm to work and sleep and try to figure out what it was that I *did* want. I even thought about leaving for good, went on a few trips to see how I felt about it, but nothing ever struck me like when I first saw that yellow house."

Noah met her gaze.

"The yellow house is why I left, and then why I stayed. I don't know if it makes sense to anyone but me but, when I'm sure about something, I think of that house and know with all of my heart it's true. For David Lapp, it was lightning, for me it was a sunflower-yellow farmhouse, and up until last week I hadn't thought about that house in a long time. That is until I saw you."

Like the epiphany he'd had when he was twelve, what he did might not have made sense to anyone else, but that wasn't going to stop him.

He'd lived a guarded, quiet life.

Now he was ready to open it up and be loud with someone.

Carly, if she'd have him.

Noah pulled a thread of silver tinsel that he'd spent a maddening amount of time fashioning into the shape of a ring from his pocket. Then he got down on his knee in front of her, the perfect height to ask for her hand.

"I didn't have time to get a ring, but I sure had

enough time to know I want to be with you, Carly. Whether that's here, there or both, I'd love it if you'd marry me."

Carly, who hadn't moved a muscle since he'd started talking, surprised him.

She laughed.

"You really do go all out, don't you? I tell you how sad I get about Christmas and here you are working overtime to make it my favorite holiday yet." She extended her fingers and eyed his makeshift ring. "Slip that on and then come up here so I can kiss you." She smiled wide. "I'd bend over but my back still hurts from getting shot."

Noah laughed.

"Yes, ma'am."

CARLY WAS IN her chair less than thirty seconds before Alana was in the briefing room, champagne in hand and barely contained glee written across her face.

"The case of the anthrax in Amish country is officially closed," she stated, her voice carrying along their makeshift dining table. It was a week later and dinner was on her, as it always was after a case well-handled. She extended her drink out before taking her own seat. "The bad guy will be in prison for a *very* long time and, thanks to some Grade-A accounting, we even tracked down Rodney's connections so we can make sure they never deal again. So here's to you, here's to us and here's to the future Noah Welsh!"

Carly burst out laughing just as the rest of the team around the table joined in.

"Does that mean he's taking my name?" Carly asked.

"Hey, I'm just saying, you were a rockstar this case," Alana added. "I mean, after all of that, *I'm* considering taking your name."

Their laughter dissolved into eating and normal chatter. Carly thumbed her new engagement ring with a sense of awe. Not at being asked to marry Noah Miller, and not at accepting without hesitation, but because no one on the team had given her any guff about it.

"I don't know," Selena had said when she'd later asked her why Selena hadn't made more of a big deal about it. "You two just kind of feel right."

Carly agreed.

It was fast. It was maybe impulsive. But it felt *right*.

Even after they'd slowed down and talked over what they both wanted at length that night in bed.

"I love my job" had been said by both, just as "I love my home" had been. Instead of that creating a problem, it had only strengthened their conviction that they would work out.

They agreed that they would split their time between Traverse City and Potter's Creek, growing roots in a straight line between the two points.

The details past that? They'd figure them out.

Together.

"You're over there smiling like a fool," Selena whispered at her ear. Carly jumped.

"And you're creeping like you're the mayor of Creep Town," she said back, swatting at her.

Selena laughed. It drew Axel's attention from his conversation with Max. He'd been looking at Selena a lot recently. If she didn't know better, Carly thought there was some tension there. Then again, maybe that was just what Selena did to some people. Most notably her sister.

That tension was noticeable and had led to many a snarky remark since being back in the same building again.

But Carly wasn't going to pry.

Not now.

Instead she was going to call her best friend a creep, drink some more champagne and think about the certain farmer who would be lying in her bed that weekend.

Not a bad Christmas after all.

* * * * *

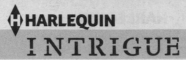

SPECIAL EXCERPT FROM

♦H HARLEQUIN
INTRIGUE

*When Raleigh Wilde reappears in
Deputy Beckett Foster's life asking for his help clearing
her name, he's shocked—even more so when he learns
she's pregnant with his child. But a killer is willing
to do anything to keep Raleigh from discovering who
embezzled millions from the charity she runs…*

Read on for a sneak preview of
The Fugitive *by Nichole Severn.*

Raleigh Wilde.

Hell, it'd been a while since Deputy United States Marshal Beckett Foster had set sights on her, and every cell in his body responded in awareness. Four months, one week and four days to be exact. Those soul-searching light green eyes, her soft brown hair and sharp cheekbones. But all that beauty didn't take away from the sawed-off shotgun currently pointed at his chest. His hand hovered just above his firearm as the Mothers Come First foundation's former chief financial officer—now fugitive—widened her stance.

"Don't you know breaking into someone's home is illegal, Marshal?" That voice. A man could get lost in a voice like that. Sweet and rough all in the same package. Raleigh smoothed her fingers over the gun in her hand. It hadn't taken her but a few seconds after she'd come through the door to realize he'd been waiting for her at the other end of the wide room.

It hadn't taken him but a couple hours to figure out where she'd been hiding for the past four months once her file crossed his desk. What she didn't know was how long he'd been waiting, and that he'd already relieved that gun of its rounds as well as any other weapons he'd found during his search of her aunt's cabin.

"Come on now. You and I both know you haven't forgotten my name that easily." He studied her from head to toe, memorizing the fit of her oversize plaid flannel shirt, the slight loss of color in her face and the dark circles under her eyes. Yeah, living on the run did that to a person. Beckett unbuttoned his holster. He wouldn't pull. Of all the criminals the United States Marshals Service had assigned him to recover over the years, she was the only one he'd hesitated chasing down. Then again, if he hadn't accepted the assignment, another marshal would have. And there was no way Beckett would let anyone else bring her in.

Beckett ran his free hand along the exposed brick of the fireplace. "Gotta be honest, didn't think you'd ever come back here. Lot of memories tied up in this place."

"What do you want, Beckett?" The creases around her eyes deepened as she shifted her weight between both feet. She crouched slightly, searching through the single window facing East Lake, then refocused on him.

Looking for a way out? Or to see if he'd come with backup? Dried grass, changing leaves, mountains and an empty dock were all that were out there. The cabin she'd been raised in as a kid sat on the west side of the lake, away from tourists, away from the main road. Even if he gave her a head start, she wouldn't get far. There was nowhere for her to run. Not from him.

"You know that, too." He took a single step forward, the aged wood floor protesting under his weight as he closed in on her. "You skipped out on your trial, and I'm here to bring you in."

"What was I supposed to do?" Countering his approach, she moved backward toward the front door she'd dead-bolted right after coming inside but kept the gun aimed at him. Her boot hit the go bag she stored near the kitchen counter beside the door. "I didn't steal that money. Someone at the charity did and faked the evidence so I'd take the fall."

"That's the best you got? A frame job?" Fifty and a half million dollars. Gone. The only one with continuous access to the funds stood right in front of him. Not to mention the brand-new offshore bank account, the thousands of wire transfers to that account in increments small enough they wouldn't register for the feds and Raleigh's signatures on every single one of them. "You had a choice, Raleigh. You just chose wrong."

Don't miss
The Fugitive *by Nichole Severn,*
available January 2021 wherever
Harlequin Intrigue books and ebooks are sold.

Harlequin.com

Get 4 FREE REWARDS!

We'll send you 2 FREE Books plus 2 FREE Mystery Gifts.

Harlequin Intrigue books are action-packed stories that will keep you on the edge of your seat. Solve the crime and deliver justice at all costs.

FREE
Value Over
$20

YES! Please send me 2 FREE Harlequin Intrigue novels and my 2 FREE gifts (gifts are worth about $10 retail). After receiving them, if I don't wish to receive any more books, I can return the shipping statement marked "cancel." If I don't cancel, I will receive 6 brand-new novels every month and be billed just $4.99 each for the regular-print edition or $5.99 each for the larger-print edition in the U.S., or $5.74 each for the regular-print edition or $6.49 each for the larger-print edition in Canada. That's a savings of at least 12% off the cover price! It's quite a bargain! Shipping and handling is just 50¢ per book in the U.S. and $1.25 per book in Canada.* I understand that accepting the 2 free books and gifts places me under no obligation to buy anything. I can always return a shipment and cancel at any time. The free books and gifts are mine to keep no matter what I decide.

Choose one: ☐ **Harlequin Intrigue**
Regular-Print
(182/382 HDN GNXC)

☐ **Harlequin Intrigue**
Larger-Print
(199/399 HDN GNXC)

Name (please print)

Address   Apt. #

City   State/Province   Zip/Postal Code

Email: Please check this box ☐ if you would like to receive newsletters and promotional emails from Harlequin Enterprises ULC and its affiliates. You can unsubscribe anytime.

Mail to the **Reader Service:**
IN U.S.A.: P.O. Box 1341, Buffalo, NY 14240-8531
IN CANADA: P.O. Box 603, Fort Erie, Ontario L2A 5X3

Want to try 2 free books from another series? Call 1-800-873-8635 or visit www.ReaderService.com.

---

*Terms and prices subject to change without notice. Prices do not include sales taxes, which will be charged (if applicable) based on your state or country of residence. Canadian residents will be charged applicable taxes. Offer not valid in Quebec. This offer is limited to one order per household. Books received may not be as shown. Not valid for current subscribers to Harlequin Intrigue books. All orders subject to approval. Credit or debit balances in a customer's account(s) may be offset by any other outstanding balance owed by or to the customer. Please allow 4 to 6 weeks for delivery. Offer available while quantities last.

Your Privacy—Your information is being collected by Harlequin Enterprises ULC, operating as Reader Service. For a complete summary of the information we collect, how we use this information and to whom it is disclosed, please visit our privacy notice located at corporate.harlequin.com/privacy-notice. From time to time we may also exchange your personal information with reputable third parties. If you wish to opt out of this sharing of your personal information, please visit readerservice.com/consumerschoice or call 1-800-873-8635. **Notice to California Residents**—Under California law, you have specific rights to control and access your data. For more information on these rights and how to exercise them, visit corporate.harlequin.com/california-privacy.

HI20R2

SPECIAL EXCERPT FROM

LOVE INSPIRED SUSPENSE
INSPIRATIONAL ROMANCE

*With his K-9's help, search and rescue K-9 handler
Patrick Sanders must find his kidnapped secret child.*

Read on for a sneak preview of
Desert Rescue *by Lisa Phillips,*
available January 2021 from Love Inspired Suspense.

"Mom!"

That had been a child's cry. State police officer Patrick
Sanders glanced across the open desert at the base of a
mountain.

Had he found what he was looking for?

Tucker sniffed, nose turned to the breeze.

Patrick's K-9 partner, an Airedale terrier he'd gotten
from a shelter as a puppy and trained, scented the wind.
His body stiffened and he leaned forward. As an air-scent
dog, Tucker didn't need a trail to follow. He could catch
the scent he was looking for on the wind or, in this case,
the winter breeze rolling over the mountain.

Patrick's mountains, the place he'd grown up. Until
right before his high school graduation when his mom
had packed them up and fled town. They'd lost their
home and everything they'd had there.

Including the girl Patrick had loved.

He heard another cry. Stifled by something—it was
hard to hear as it drifted across so much open terrain.

He and his K-9 had been dispatched to find Jennie and her son, Nathan. A friend had reported them missing yesterday, and the sheriff wasted no time at all calling for a search and rescue team from state police.

The dog had caught a scent and was closing in.

As a terrier, it was about the challenge. Tucker had proved to be both prey-driven, like fetching a ball, and food-driven, like a nice piece of chicken, when he felt like it.

Right now the dog had to find Jennie and the boy so Patrick could transport them to safety. Then he intended to get out of town again. Back to his life in Albuquerque and studying for the sergeant's exam.

Tucker tugged harder on the leash; a signal the scent was stronger. He was closing in. Patrick's night of searching for the missing woman and her child would soon be over.

Tucker rounded a sagebrush and sat.

"Good boy. Yes, you are." Patrick let the leash slacken a little. He circled his dog and found Jennie lying on the ground.

"Jennie."

She stirred. Her eyes flashed open and she cried out. *"We need to find Nate."*

Don't miss
Desert Rescue *by Lisa Phillips,*
available wherever Love Inspired Suspense books and ebooks are sold.

LoveInspired.com